# Flights, Fights, & Christmas Lights

LoLo Paige

Published by Avoca Press Publishing, 2024.

# Chapter 1



The commuter plane bumped to a landing on the snowy Talkeetna Airstrip. Sadie Foster gripped her phone, willing herself to relax. She'd flown to Alaska two days ahead of her fiancé to indulge in the Denali Roadhouse Lodge's famous spa, especially their Nordic hot tubs where guests could choose their perfect temperature.

She climbed out of her seat, excited to hear the flight attendant's cheerful announcement: "Welcome to Talkeetna!" The frigid air hit her face as she descended the stairs to the snowy airstrip, carrying with it the scent of winter and aviation fuel. Her designer boots, chosen for their style rather than practicality, slipped on the icy tarmac.

Sadie followed the rest of the passengers to a small building to collect her bags. It took a while for both her bags to appear on the petite conveyor belt. When they did, she piled them onto a pushcart and headed over to the ground transportation desk.

As she was about to contact the car she'd booked with Uber, her phone buzzed. She glanced down to see a text from Clayton. She smiled. He must be getting ready to fly up here tomorrow.

Sadie tapped the text.

*Hey, beautiful! Loved spending the night before last with you. Been thinking about that thing you do with your tongue. Hope your husband doesn't suspect anything. I'm free tonight before I fly up to Alaska tomorrow. Drive over to my place. XOXO Clayton.*

Sadie blinked. She read the text three times, her stomach growing icier with each pass. Ever since Thanksgiving, Clayton had to work late and went out of town on weekends, but she'd not given it a second thought. Never in her wildest imagination did she think he was cheating.

This certainly was a bolt out of the blue. Especially when they'd been planning for weeks to spend the Christmas holiday in a cozy Alaskan cabin.

She froze, debating how to respond to her fiancé's message intended for someone else. Sadie wondered who it was, then she recalled an overly friendly blonde who'd shown up at Clayton's office party a few weeks ago. Sadie had shrugged it off, assuming they worked together. Apparently, they did a heck of a lot more than that.

After pondering the situation, Sadie typed out what she considered a thoughtful response:

*This is your ex-fiancée. Wrong number, asshole! Don't bother flying up to Alaska unless you want moose turds thrown in your face. P.S. I'm selling your diamond ring. (smiley face)*

She topped it off with a gif of a woman repeatedly flipping the bird.

Sadie switched off her phone before he could reply and stood in the middle of the building. She didn't bother hiding her forlorn expression as she pondered what to do next. She absolutely had to get back on that airplane! She watched in dismay as the last passengers boarded the flight back to Anchorage. Then the ramp lifted, and the door closed.

"No!" she hollered. Every head turned toward her as she flew out the door, waving her arms. "Wait! I need to get back on!"

The propellors were already spinning, drowning out her voice. She watched helplessly as the aircraft taxied away, leaving her stranded in this tiny Alaska town with her shattered dreams and impractical footwear.

Disappointed, she shuffled back inside the one-horse air terminal to ask about the next flight to Anchorage.

A perky young woman glanced up from her computer. "Next flight to Anchorage isn't until the day after tomorrow. They run every other day. There's a storm on the way, anyway."

"Not today? Not tomorrow?" Sadie's voice cracked. "What is this, the boonies? There must be an earlier flight."

"I can get you there," a voice piped up behind her.

Sadie turned to find a stout, smiling man in a worn pilot's cap, ear flaps hanging down. He extended a leather-gloved hand. "Lucky O'Hara. Preparing to fly to Anchorage as we speak." His voice dripped Irish like an overfilled pint of Guinness.

Sadie hesitated, then shook his hand. "Sadie Foster. You're sure about the weather?" She peeked out the window at a small red plane with two white stripes running along the fuselage.

"Been flying these routes for twenty years." His Irish lilt carried a note of pride. "I'll get us above the worst of it with my DeHavilland Beaver."

Twenty minutes later, Sadie white-knuckled the passenger seat of Lucky's red ski plane as they ascended into the swirling snowstorm. The aircraft seemed solid enough, but having only one propellor made her heart skip a beat. Especially in this whiteout, where she couldn't get her bearings.

"Might get a wee bit bouncy, but don't worry, The Beave can handle it!" Lucky shouted over the engine noise, banking hard to the right. "Storm's moving fast and taller than expected."

Sadie's stomach lurched as they hit a deep air pocket. Outside her window, white peaks pierced the clouds like jagged teeth waiting to devour them. The aircraft shuddered violently as the pilot wrangled the insistent snow for a good fifteen minutes.

"Can't get above her." He flicked the altimeter with his forefinger, but the jiggling was too intense for Sadie to get a read on the numbers. The single-engine dipped hard to the left and her stomach flopped over to the port side along with it.

"Change of plans, Miss Sadie," Lucky announced cheerfully. "Got to set down in Polar Creek to wait this out."

"Polar what?" Sadie's question ended in a shriek as the DeHavilland Beaver plummeted again. She frantically searched for anything to lock onto besides the thick curtain of snowflakes.

He gave her a sideways glance. "Don't worry, I got her under control." His voice jiggled as the bush plane shuddered.

"Where's this Polar place?" She pressed her forehead to the glass in the passenger seat. She saw nothing.

"You'll see it any second now—there!" The bush pilot dipped his head to the side.

Through the relentless blizzard, Sadie glimpsed a cluster of buildings, their windows glowing like warm jewels in the gathering dusk. Like a mirage, everything disappeared when the plane bucked again, her feet lifting off the floor.

"Quite the crosswind!" Lucky's voice remained impossibly upbeat as they descended. "Hold tight. Might be a rough landing."

Everything was a flat white, and Sadie couldn't see anything resembling a town. She couldn't tell where the ground was, so she squeezed her eyes shut, mentally composing her own epitaph: "Here lies Sadie, who died in a flying tin can with a crazy Irishman in the Alaskan wilderness because her cheating fiancé couldn't keep his texts straight."

The wheeled skis hit the snow with a bone-jarring thud, and Sadie bit her tongue. The aircraft bounced once, twice, then skidded sideways. She braced herself, expecting this DeHavilland Beaver to roll over when it finally skidded to a stop. Her heart still raced, even after the propellor fell silent.

"Welcome to Polar Creek!" Lucky announced, the howling wind lifting the wings, still jostling them around. "Population one hundred and twelve. Thirteen now, counting you."

Nursing her sore tongue, Sadie's response was a sound between a laugh and a sob. Outside, the storm howled its triumph, and the heavy flakes picked up speed, threatening to bury them alive as they sat in the ski plane. All she saw was white.

Everywhere.

Fantastic. Not only had her fiancé cheated on her, she'd landed inside of a mother freaking snow globe that some joker had shaken.

To make matters worse, her cell phone displayed zero bars.

# Chapter 2

K*reston*

Kreston Collins cut the engine of his aging snowmachine and squinted through the blowing white at Lucky's zig-zagging aircraft as it came in a little wonky, then landed on skis, bouncing over the snow. He'd cleared most of the snow with his truck plow when Lucky told him he'd be setting down in Polar Creek instead of Anchorage.

Lucky's landing was rougher than usual, and Kreston winced—no surprise, given the heavy crosswinds whipping down from the Alaska Range. He shook his head at his best buddy's piloting ability. He wasn't a risk taker, but when the going got dicey, Lucky was skilled enough to not only keep his bird in the air but to set it down safely in one piece.

Lucky liked to brag, "I've never left The Beave up there yet!"

Kreston, also a bush pilot, was amused at his friend's nickname for his plane, along with his offhanded Irish humor.

Lucky had radioed him about a diverted passenger, a Seattle woman in a hurry to get to Anchorage. Now she'd be stuck here until the storm passed, which wouldn't be for several days according to the forecast. Not this time of year, when the powerful Bering Sea lows spun through the state, whipping up snow like a McDonald's McFlurry stuck on whir.

# FLIGHTS, FIGHTS, & CHRISTMAS LIGHTS

Kreston blew out air and stepped out of his truck, trudging through the drifts toward the DeHavilland Beaver, cursing himself for forgetting his snowshoes. He braced himself for the inevitable complaints from another entitled tourist about the lack of cell service and gourmet coffee. Especially those from Seattle, who claimed their city made the best espresso drinks worldwide, even better than the Italians.

Kreston disagreed with that premise. He'd spent time in Italy, and there was no comparison.

"Quite the landing, wasn't it?" Lucky greeted him as he climbed from the pilot seat and jumped into the snow. "Reminds me of that time in Tok when we had to get those hunters out."

"Which time? The one where you gave me a heart attack or the other time where you gave me a worse heart attack?" quipped Kreston, grinning at his buddy. "How'd those new wheeled skis work for you?"

"Like a lucky charm." Lucky grinned and moved in close. "I brought you an early Christmas present. Don't say I never gave you anything." He elbowed Kreston in the ribs and winked, which Kreston knew to be trouble.

Dreading what or who he would find, Kreston moved around the tail to the passenger door and flung it open.

He momentarily forgot the cold upon seeing the drop-dead gorgeous woman riding shotgun in the passenger seat. Auburn curls cascaded in waves from her wool headband, a stark contrast in the dim light like red maple leaves in the fall. Her eyes were a striking shade of amber-gold. Despite her obvious distress, something about her caught his attention—the determined set of her jaw, or maybe it was the way she held herself like she was ready for battle. She looked like a person none too happy with her new surroundings and intended to let everyone know about it.

The woman who swung her shapely bare legs to climb out of the airplane took his breath away. Not because of her good looks—that was a given—but what the heck was she doing in an impossibly short dress and a short suede jacket in this ungodly snowy weather? It had been a long while since Kreston was a fashion maven, but he seemed to remember one didn't wear suede in a flipping snowstorm.

Not only that, she also wore the most impractical boots Kreston had ever seen in Alaska. Brown thigh-high patent leather boots with five, no, six-inch heels? The wind whipped her hair around her face, and for a moment, she resembled an actress on a movie set—beautiful, fierce, and completely out of place.

"Hello, I'm Kreston Collins. Welcome to Polar Creek," he said smoothly in his hotel manager's voice. It was rare to see visitors during a hellacious winter snowstorm.

Lucky slapped his shoulder. "Kreston is also our mayor. And our postal carrier. Not to mention one of the best bush pilots I know."

Kreston caught the woman's surprise. "Small town. We wear multiple hats here."

"Right. How quaint." Her glare could melt permafrost. "Mr. Collins, where in the heck is Polar Creek?" she tossed out, none too friendly.

"On the other side of Denali Park, a dozen miles west of the park boundary. I didn't catch your name."

"Because I didn't give it." Her words were clipped and laced with aggravation. "I won't be staying. I need to get to Anchorage as soon as the weather allows."

"Her name is Sadie Foster," Lucky happily provided. "Did you know she's a big-shot publicist in Seattle? She handles celebrity clients, like the Seattle Seahawks and the Mariners—"

"Lucky, chill," warned Kreston, appreciating his buddy's good intentions. In the time it took to fly her here, Lucky had probably learned Sadie's entire life story. The man could chat with a fence post and get its autobiography in thirty seconds.

"Just thought you'd like to know." Lucky grinned, his eyes crinkling.

Kreston offered Sadie his thick-gloved hand to help her from the passenger seat.

"Thank you," she said in a business-like tone.

Lucky turned to Sadie. "Did I mention Kreston here is quite the eligible bachelor—"

"Lucky, chill!" interjected Kreston, giving his friend the eye. "No one cares."

"I'm not in the market," Sadie cut in, her voice sharp enough to slice glaciers.

Kreston bit back a smile as he opened the cargo door. He grunted, hoisting two huge, heavy bags. "Yours, I presume?" he asked Sadie.

"Oh, those can't get wet," she said quickly, her amber hair sticking to her face along with the snowflakes.

"They'll have to ride in the back with you, then." Kreston considered offering her the front seat, but he didn't appreciate her attitude. He carried her bags to the pickup and heaved them into one side of the back seat, then opened the door on the opposite side.

"Get in. You aren't exactly dressed for this weather," he said.

"Who are you to tell me how to dress?" she spat at him. "I'm doing just fine, thank you very much."

Lovely. A woman full of piss and vinegar. She lifted a leg to climb unsuccessfully inside his tall pickup and grunted as she tried to get in.

"I'll do the honors," he mumbled, grabbing her by the waist and lifting her into the back seat, where she glared down at him. "Get a good look?"

"Regretfully, no." He slammed the rear door closed and rounded the front of his pickup. "Not something I'm into with snow stinging my face," he grumbled, his hair whipping like a tornado had hold of it. He opened the driver's door, slid into the seat, and sat back.

"What are we waiting for?" Sadie asked impatiently.

Kreston didn't reply. Instead, he pointed to Lucky, putting the Beave to bed inside the two-plane hangar the two friends built a few summers ago.

"Oh." She said it as if he'd insulted her.

Kreston thought the best course of action was not to say much of anything.

Lucky hopped into the front passenger seat, and Kreston shifted into four-wheel drive for the two miles into town.

"Forecast says the storm will intensify." Kreston glanced at Lucky. "Supposed to snow for the next four days."

"No!" Sadie yelled from the back seat, her expression darkening like the storm clouds. "There must be a way to get to Anchorage!"

"Not unless you have a dog team hidden in your designer bag." Kreston turned on his brights in the waning light, then looked in the rearview mirror. "No roads between here and Anchorage. Good thing Lucky diverted you here when he did."

"Yes, he's quite the hero," she bit out. "Maybe you should write him up for a medal in your capacity as mayor. Or do you handle that as a hotel manager? Hard to keep track of your many royal titles."

*Wow, this woman was a piece of work. Remind me never to go to another big city if this is what most women are like these days.*

Sheets of white swirled around them on the drive to town, which was treacherous but silent except for the howl of wind and the truck's engine. Lucky fell asleep, and Kreston was stealing glances in the rearview at his passenger, noting how she stared straight ahead, giving off a "don't talk to me" vibe.

He speculated on what put those shadows in her eyes and the defensive edge in her voice. Not that it was any of his concern. Kreston was aware of his passenger's white-knuckled grip on the wimp handle. "So, you're up from Seattle?"

"Yes." She wasn't exactly long-winded. At least she wouldn't talk him to death.

"Welcome to Alaska," he said, for lack of anything else to say. Something told him she felt anything but welcome. He might have been sympathetic if she wasn't so cantankerous.

As they crested the hill overlooking town, the Polar Creek Hotel came into view, its windows glowing amber against the intense storm. The two-story log building stood like a sentinel in the swirling snow, smoke curling from its stone chimney into the darkening sky.

"There's your digs." A hint of pride laced his words. "Been here since 1947, and it even has indoor plumbing."

"How up to date." Her voice dripped with icicles.

He sucked in a breath. This woman could prove difficult to get along with.

"Well, you know, we try to keep up with the times."

Lucky's loud snores stopped when Kreston cut the engine after parking in front of the Polar Creek Hotel. Through the windows, he noted how the massive stone fireplace cast a warm glow around the lobby. Several people relaxed in the mismatched armchairs around the crackling fire, and the Gossip Trio were no doubt trading juicy stories while enjoying Jessie Thompson's fresh-baked sourdough slices.

The scent of wood smoke and baking bread met Kreston as he opened the door. He detected the ghost of a smile Sadie quickly suppressed. She was pretty when she wasn't scowling. More than pretty, if he was being honest—which he wouldn't be, because she was trouble, wrapped in impractical boots and a suede coat ruined by wet snowflakes.

"It's blowing hard. Go ahead inside, and I'll get your bags," he said.

"I don't need protection from a little snow." Sadie stiffened but didn't move away. "You're a porter too? I don't need help with my bags." She grabbed one and tried to roll it through knee-high snowdrifts, the wheels spinning helplessly into the powdery white mounds.

"Suit yourself." Kreston grabbed the mailbag Lucky had flown in.

Sadie rolled her eyes. "Is there anything in this town you don't do?"

"I don't make espresso drinks," he said over his shoulder. "In case you were wondering."

"Never said I wanted one." Her voice could frost windowpanes.

Kreston figured she was the type who always had to have the last word. He felt sorry for her boyfriend, whoever the poor schmuck was. He'd heard Lucky say something on the radio about a cheating ex. He could see why.

He watched her struggle with the luggage until he couldn't take it anymore. Rolling his eyes, he strode outside and grabbed the heaviest bag from her hand.

Her feet slid out from under her, and his instant reflex caught her before she went down.

"Careful," he cautioned, gripping her waist with one hand and her bag with the other. "It's slippery out here in the wilderness."

Their eyes met for a moment, and she stiffened.

"Thank you for the fascinating insight into Arctic physics." This woman might be abrasive, but she sure didn't let go of his arm.

"Last chance to camp in the snow if this is too rustic for you." He hadn't had a woman hang onto him like this in a good while, and he kind of liked it. Jeez, was he that hard up?

The double doors burst open, and a tall, big-boned woman with a yellow bun called out, "About time you got here. Thought your truck got buried. We were about to send out a search party."

Lucky woke up, yawned, and tugged up the waistband of his tan Carhartts. "Couldn't get these two to stop ogling each other. Glad we made it, though." He gave Jessie a quick wink as she held the hotel door open, and he stumbled inside.

"No, we didn't! Is he always like this?" asked Sadie, exasperation in her voice as she pointed a thumb at Lucky.

"Lucky? Nah." Kreston shook his head, guiding her toward the door. "Usually, he's much worse."

Kreston's dear friend turned to Sadie. "Hello, I'm Jessie Thompson. I run the Crooked Spoon bar and restaurant here in the hotel." She gave a subtle nod in the general direction.

Once inside, Sadie released Kreston's arm and marched to the check-in desk, her designer boots clicking against the wooden floors. He caught himself watching how the firelight softened her face as she took in the lobby's warm glow. Her gaze lingered on the enormous fireplace and the guests scattered across worn sofas and chairs, all of them lounging like they were in their own living rooms.

The scene delighted him, and he smiled. This was exactly the authentic wilderness charm he'd envisioned when he took over the hotel. Creaky spruce-hewn floors stretched beneath thick woolen rugs, while vintage oil lamps cast a gentle glow over the local artwork and mounted antlers adorning the log walls. The whole place felt like a cozy wilderness retreat, exactly as he'd intended.

Something in Sadie's expression caught his attention—a flash of vulnerability that made her look like she was nursing a fresh wound. He wondered what had brought that shadow to her eyes, then quickly dismissed the thought. Whatever her story was, it wasn't his business. The last thing he needed was another complication in his already overfull life.

Any warmth in the moment vanished when Kreston stepped behind the reception counter.

"Don't tell me you're also the check-in clerk?" She said it like she was annoyed by it.

He'd wanted to make things easier by checking her into a room, but her attitude made him reconsider. "I'll have Aloha check you in."

"Excuse me? Aloha?" Her perfectly shaped eyebrows arched in disbelief.

He couldn't help but enjoy her bewildered expression. "Yes, Aloha."

"I'm sure my plane landed in Alaska, not Hawaii," she snorted, making a pretense of glancing around. "Do you have actual rooms, or should I just curl up by the fire for a cozy pajama party?" She gestured toward the crackling flames in the massive stone fireplace.

"Depends." He paused, savoring the moment. "For visitors, we try to manage something resembling a bed instead of the usual ropes and straw we normally have available. For you, we'll even toss in a few modern conveniences at no extra charge."

"How generous." Her words could have etched glass.

*What is this woman's problem?*

Kreston eyed her ruined suede leather jacket, a mottled brown-gray mess from the wet snow. "Interesting fashion choice. Channeling your inner *Maverick* from *Top Gun*, or is grunge making a comeback in Seattle?"

She glanced down at her sodden jacket, then flicked her eyes up at him. "Sorry to disappoint, but I left my F-18 Super Hornet parked at Pike Place Market with my grunge band."

Quick-witted. He'd give her that.

This storm was stacking up to be a long one, and if he had a lick of sense, he'd stop noticing things—like the glint in her eyes when she was irritated, or how her legs seemed to stretch forever from under that short skirt and those impossible boots.

The storm howled outside, settling in like it planned to stay a while. Kreston had a feeling it wasn't the only force of nature he'd be contending with in the days ahead.

# Chapter 3



Sadie's momentary guilt over her behavior vanished when Kreston passed her off to the front desk clerk, looking relieved to be finally rid of her.

"I have to check on Ten Second Tess before she reorganizes the supply closet again. Last time, we found the red towels in the freezer because she needed to cool them down." He strode off across the sizeable lobby and disappeared into a dimly lit hallway.

Sadie didn't know what to think and stared after him, baffled.

A woman with wild black hair appeared, wearing a Hawaiian shirt, flip-flops, and board shorts. In Alaska. In December. She stepped behind the reception desk and beamed a toothy grin at Sadie. She fiddled with a partially decorated Christmas tree perched on the counter, covered with miniature soap and shampoo bottles, hotel keys, and toilet paper draped around it like garland. Then she picked up a deck of cards and expertly shuffled them. Repeatedly.

"Aloha! Welcome to Polar Creek Hotel. I'm Aloha." Her toothy smile could serve as a backup generator to the building's electricity, since the power had blinked a 'hello' and a 'how are you' the minute Sadie came through the door.

Sadie's confusion must have been obvious because the woman dove into further details.

"Aloha means hello and goodbye, but it's also my name." She thought for a minute, staring at the ceiling. "It's probably not my actual name. Though I really don't know." She leaned across the counter and whispered. "None of us are sure." She shuffled the cards, then tapped the deck on the counter like a Vegas poker dealer.

Sadie blinked. "You're not sure what your name is?"

Kreston's voice came out of nowhere from behind, causing Sadie to jump. "Found Aloha in an Anchorage Costco parking lot five years ago," he explained, holding a tower of red towels.

"He really did. God bless him." Aloha's hands moved with practiced grace as she shuffled the deck, her fingers cutting the cards, then fanning them across the counter in a precise arc.

Kreston leaned on the counter with his stack of towels. "Complete amnesia. She said her name was 'aloha,' so that's what we called her. Brought her to Polar Creek since she had no place to go. Costco hated to see her leave since she did such a great job rounding up the shopping carts." A smile tipped the corners of his mouth, and he hurried up a set of wide, creaky stairs.

With his winter gear off, Sadie couldn't help but notice his toned physique. Broad shoulders narrowing to a slender waist. Without meaning to, she watched his cute hiney move up the stairs along with the rest of him.

"Cute, isn't he? Wish I could marry him," sighed Aloha with a dreamy look, her chin resting on her hand.

"You mean he just took you home, like a stray dog?" Sadie inadvertently recalled the spoiled and entitled celebrity who'd hired her to organize a city-wide search for her lost chihuahua. Sadie had secretly hoped it'd found its way into another woman's oversized designer bag.

Aloha laughed. "For some reason, I remembered how to make a Mai Tai. I'll make you one sometime." She leaned across the counter again and whispered, "Kreston says I'm not allowed to serve alcohol before noon. Or maybe he means noon somewhere else? I forget." She wrinkled her face in thought, then picked up the card deck and shuffled.

Sadie was desperate for privacy, to unwind and relax. She was bone tired. She also had a few choice things to say to her cheating ex-fiancé.

"I'd like a room, please. Just for tonight." The last words came out as a desperate plea.

A woman breezed up, who looked to be in her forties. Thick brown hair hung in a French braid down to her waist. She flipped it behind her and tapped Sadie's shoulder, then quickly backed up.

"Want to help me finish decorating the Christmas tree?" she chirped. "I keep forgetting which decorations I've already put up."

Sadie's eyes flicked to the tree on the counter. "They're right here."

When she turned back to the woman, she'd vanished. People came and went so quickly here.

*Did this one also have amnesia? Doesn't anyone remember anything around here? I've either landed in Oz or in the movie "One Flew Over the Cuckoo's Nest!"*

"Don't mind her, she's Ten Second Tess. Her memory is worse than mine." Aloha's chin rested in her hand as she leaned on the counter. "Now, what were we doing?"

"My room?" said Sadie, nearly pleading.

"Oh, yes! I remember. I love saying 'I remember' because everything was a blur before Costco—"

A crash from upstairs interrupted, followed by Kreston's voice. "Tess, we talked about this—the miniature soaps go inside the hotel rooms on the bathroom sink counters. Not inside the ice machine. There's no need to keep them cold."

"What's a sink counter?" the woman with the braid hollered back. "And where's the ice machine?"

Sadie's brows winged up. *What kind of crazytown did she land in?*

"Ten Second Tess had a brain injury that robbed her of memory," explained Aloha. "She hangs onto things for only ten minutes at a time, but it seems like ten seconds, so we call her Ten Second Tess. Then she resets." Aloha laughed. "I don't remember much before Polar Creek, but at least I can hang onto things longer than ten minutes."

"Lots of memory loss around here. Hope it's not catching," muttered Sadie. She wanted to crawl into a bear's den and emerge when this nightmare was over. She pinched the bridge of her nose.

"Please tell me you at least have Wi-Fi."

"Sure do! And the password is *krestonissingle*." She said it slowly and emphatically. "All lowercase, no underscores or spaces." She leaned across the check-in counter and whispered, "Kreston's muscles aren't just for show. They're very real. Not that I've been looking. Well, maybe I have. You know how it is...more men than women in Alaska." She beamed another smile, picked up her deck, and shuffled.

Sadie fought for composure. "The password is, Kreston is single? Seriously?"

*What's with the people in this town? Why are they desperate to get Kreston hooked up?*

Now she was suspicious of the guy. Was there something wrong with him? Did he have memory loss too? He seemed normal enough, but Sadie wasn't always spot on with first impressions.

Aloha chortled. "Good luck with the internet access. It blinks on and off like the Christmas lights, so if it blinks off, just smack the little box in your room, and that sucker will fire right up." She tapped Sadie's arm. "Did I mention our mayor is single? He's a good bush pilot, too."

Sadie gave her an incredulous look. "Yes, you mentioned the single thing."

Aloha drew back with a frown. "What single thing? Is that like a double thing?"

Sadie gave her a blank look. "No, you said—" She stopped. "Never mind. Please, just give me the room key," she pleaded.

"What key? Oh! Here you go." Aloha handed over a metal key attached to a large, hand-carved wooden moose. "Room 204 has the best view of the Aurora Borealis when it's not snowing sideways. Breakfast starts at seven in the Crooked Spoon. Jessie makes delicious sourdough pancakes, and they'll make you forget all about that cheating fiancé of yours."

Sadie nearly dropped the moose. "How did you—?"

"Lucky radioed ahead from The Beave after you guys landed." Aloha laughed and shook her head. "Honestly, he's worse than CNN about broadcasting breaking news. I gave you the Wi-Fi password, right?"

"Yes, but uh—"

*Please God, get me out of here.*

"Love your boots, by the way." Aloha offered her a knowing girlfriend grin. "Totally impractical for Alaska, but your legs look amazing. Not that I noticed, but I noticed that Kreston noticed. Not that he said anything, you understand. Upstairs and to the left." She pointed again. "Where you from again? Did I give you the password?" She put a finger to her chin and looked up at the ceiling as if it would answer her.

Kreston tapped down the stairs. "Sucks about your cheating ex. I'll help you with your bags."

"How did you—how does everyone know? I only told that airplane pilot." Sadie didn't mean to sound rude, but she was spent. "Sorry, but I don't have cash for a tip."

"Not doing it for cash." With ease, he lifted both bags as if they were empty and climbed the stairs.

A deck of cards shuffled behind Sadie as she muscled her loaded carry-on up the creaky steps, clunking it on each one up to the second-floor carpeted hallway. She couldn't help noticing the worn carpet decorated with miniature airplanes as she rolled her carry-on. Kreston stepped aside as she shoved her key into the lock, the oversized moose bumping against the door.

Kreston wheeled the bags inside her room and stood in the center. "Where do you want these?"

Sadie noticed the bunching of his arm muscles when he lifted her bag. She told herself she wouldn't be here long enough to notice anything else—she wouldn't stay any longer than she had to in this bizarre twilight zone of a time warp.

"Doesn't matter." Too exhausted to care, she vaguely motioned to a corner.

He hoisted one oversized bag onto a worn wooden luggage holder. "Holy smokes, hope this thing can hold it. Looks like half of Seattle came up here with you." He peered at the wobbly luggage holder.

"I've never been to Alaska," she said defensively. "I didn't know what to pack."

"Well, if you need anything, let me or Aloha know." He took the key from the lock and handed it to her. "Here's your moose. Have a good evening." He closed the door behind him to return to whatever it was he did. The guy seemed to pop up everywhere.

Sadie glanced around with hands on her hips. The room was surprisingly charming, and it was clean. A thick quilt with embroidered squares of moose, ravens, and caribou rested on the bed. An overstuffed armchair sat in one corner with a cute round table next to it, topped with a caribou lamp. The furniture was rustic but solid. She'd traveled back in time like in a sci-fi movie. If this room could talk, she was sure it would have tall tales to tell.

"Quaint, but I'm not staying," Sadie muttered out loud. She thought of next week's back-to-back meeting schedule after the holidays with her damaged, wealthy clientele. The only time they had memory issues was when they were caught sleeping with a best friend's wife or were recorded on CCTV buying and using illegal drugs.

She shed her ruined expensive suede jacket, and her stomach roiled. Why had she worn this? Remembering, she grimaced and rolled her eyes. Because Clayton told her it was sexy.

"Good! I'm glad you're ruined now!" she shouted at the helpless jacket. So what if she was out a thousand bucks?

Irritated, Sadie fired up her phone. Great, no cell service. Probably because of the storm, which rattled the windows like it was poking fun at her plans.

She did her before-bed routine and slid under the sheet and heavy comforter. Sleep came right away, with dreams of blue-eyed mayors and Hawaiian shirts in snowstorms.

# Chapter 4

S*adie*
A knock at the door interrupted her cozy dream. Unable to remember where she was, she popped one eye open. Yep—still in this nightmare. It wasn't a bad dream after all, as she'd hoped.

"Housekeeping!" called out a chipper voice. "I need to clean this room!"

"No—not yet—what time is it?" Sadie hollered back.

No answer, only muffled voices in the hallway.

"Tess!" Kreston's patient voice came from down the hall. "Let her sleep. She had a rough day yesterday."

"What's her name? I have to clean the room, Mayor Kreston! Did you know we have a guest from New York? Did I miss Christmas? Where is New York, anyway?"

"Her name is Sadie, and she's from Seattle. No, you didn't miss Christmas, and New York may as well be on another planet," he explained, as if talking to a child. "Please take the soaps and shampoos out of the ice maker. We don't store them there, remember?"

Telling a person with severe memory problems to remember was like walking backwards up Mount Denali, thought Sadie as she lay on her back, listening.

As the voices faded, Sadie wondered what she had wandered into. Now that she was fully awake, she crawled out of the surprisingly comfortable bed and wandered into the bathroom. She warily eyed the shower and turned the handles. Nothing happened. She spun the handles again, and still nothing happened.

Sadie wandered out of the tiny bathroom and let out a frustrated sigh. As she unzipped one of her large bags, a sudden burst of water sounded from the bathroom.

"Finally!" she muttered, stepping in to see a steady brown stream coming out of the shower nozzle. "No, not dirty water!" she yelled.

There was no phone in her room to call the reception desk, and her phone still had no cell bars. Great. She'd have to get dressed, go downstairs, and demand a room with clean water.

Sadie stomped back into the bathroom to find clean water shooting out of the nozzle. All traces of brown had gone down the drain. She stepped into the shower, grateful for the intense pressure massaging her skin. In fact, it was almost too hard, but compared to no water or brown water, she'd take it.

After showering, she pawed through her bag and took out a pair of fleece-lined leggings and her heaviest wool socks. She searched her other large bag on the floor to find her ankle boots with stiletto heels, slightly more sensible than her thigh highs with six-inch heels. She tossed on a heavy sweater over a t-shirt, slicked her wet hair back into a sleek ponytail, and headed for the door. She grabbed the moose key and let herself out to the hallway and down the stairs with one aim in mind: coffee.

Kreston was in his winter gear, but before she could call out to him, he'd disappeared out the door. This guy always seemed on the go. Where on earth did he get his energy?

# FLIGHTS, FIGHTS, & CHRISTMAS LIGHTS

Sadie moved toward the Crooked Spoon restaurant and bar on the hotel's first floor, a cozy space, more like an oversized kitchen than a restaurant. A massive copper-topped bar dominated one wall, its surface burnished by years of elbows and coffee cups. Mismatched tables filled the room, each topped with a mason jar of pine branches and twinkling lights.

One corner housed an ancient wood-burning stove, radiating heat and nostalgia. Ink sketches of mountain landscapes and wildlife in hand-hewn wood frames dotted the walls. Garlands of evergreen wrapped the exposed beams overhead, and someone had arranged Christmas cards from what looked like decades of past guests along the windowsills.

It was still pitch-black outside but the seven a.m. breakfast crowd filled every available booth and table, their conversations creating a warm hum beneath the clatter of plates and silverware.

Every head turned in Sadie's direction when she entered and stood looking for a seat. Then the heads leaned together to gab in low voices, stealing looks at her. Okay, she was the new fish-out-of-water attraction in a small town.

"Well, look what the storm blew in!" Jessie's bottle-blonde hair was in another messy bun. "You're skin and bones. Get over here and have a bite." She tapped a chair at the only empty table, and the smell of fresh bread and coffee beckoned Sadie to take her up on it.

"I would appreciate a cup of coffee. Please," Sadie politely added as she sat down. A twinge poked her chest after her grouchy behavior yesterday. She felt the need to explain.

"I'm really not a jerk, despite what some might think. It's just that—well, I got dumped and then stranded in this flipping Alaskan time warp. No offense," she added quickly.

"None taken." Jessie held a coffeepot and turned over a sizeable mug. "Here you go. Then I'll talk you into my sourdough pancakes. Been feeding my starter, which is older than you've been alive. Got it from a lady now deceased, who won it in a poker game from a sourdough miner back in 1942."

Too much information. Sadie held up her hand in a stop motion. "No, thank you. Not a pancake eater."

"We'll see about that." Jessie dashed off.

"It's useless. Don't fight it." A bald man with a brown beard and a green plaid flannel shirt shuffled to her table, eyes crinkling behind wire-rimmed glasses. "Jessie will spoon feed you those pancakes unless you give in. Mind if I sit?"

Sadie motioned to a chair across the table. "Sure, have a seat. And thanks for the tip."

"Jessie's pancakes are a comfort to the mind and soul." He pulled out a chair and lowered himself into it with the slowness of a man Sadie guessed to be eighty. "These days, I pay in sketches. Fire insurance, as it turns out, doesn't cover vengeful ex-wives with matches."

Sadie chose to leave that one alone. Instead, she looked around for a menu. Not seeing one, she sipped her coffee, waiting for Jessie to return.

He extended his hand. "Tucker Sweet. Former artist, contemporary poet, self-appointed philosopher, and perpetual admirer of the Alaskan way of life."

She shook his hand. "Sadie Foster from Seattle. Current hostage of Polar Creek, and not a fan of snow and small towns."

"Ah, but snow in Alaska isn't just snow," Tucker mused. "It's nature's way of forcing us to slow down, to see the beauty in stillness. Like when I was painting the northern lights and became so mesmerized by the dancing colors, I didn't notice my easel had frozen to the ground. Kreston saved the day by chipping it free with an ice pick. That boy has the patience of a saint and the stubbornness of a moose."

"Does every story in this town involve Kreston?" The words came out sharper than intended, her defenses rising at the mere mention of his name.

"Most of them," Jessie chimed in, sliding a plate of golden pancakes in front of Sadie. "The man's got a heart bigger than Alaska. I should know—he found me crying in an Anchorage restaurant and brought me here. Next thing I knew, I had a fresh start running this place." She paused, her expression warm with memory. "Kreston has a knack for knowing what people need before they figure it out themselves."

"Sounds like he has a habit of collecting strays. Thank you, but honestly, I don't eat pancakes," she said weakly, eying the wild blueberry compote and freshly whipped cream resembling a snow-capped peak.

Jessie only smiled and dashed off to refill empty mugs with coffee.

"Kreston has done his share of saving those running from things bigger than themselves," Tucker said quietly, his artistic eye scrutinizing her.

Sadie gave him a direct look. "I don't need saving and I'm not running. Just inconvenienced by weather and poor cell reception." She clamped her mouth shut before adding a scathing remark about her cheating fiancé.

Had she stumbled into the land of misfit toys, like that old Christmas cartoon? For all she knew, Kreston was an undercover Santa, complete with reindeer and a sleigh secretly stashed behind the Polar Creek Hotel.

Lucky O'Hara and Kreston ambled into the Crooked Spoon, Kreston's coat draped casually over one arm. Sadie couldn't help noticing how his Norwegian-knit sweater hugged his broad shoulders and chest. The room erupted in greetings to both. Everyone carried on as if welcoming the lead singers of the Middle-of-Nowhere Alaska Band, back from their world tour.

Sadie's eye caught Kreston's, and he smiled as he headed to her table. "Loving the sourdough, I see?" He stood grinning at her.

Lucky took the chair next to Tucker. "Miss Sadie, the weather report just came in, straight from the moose's mouth."

Sadie paused with her forkful of pancakes in midair, hoping for a weather miracle.

"The forecast is for endless snow. Around here we call such weather shitty to partly shitty." Lucky beamed. "But don't worry—you're in the best place to wait out a storm."

# Chapter 5



Sadie stabbed at her pancakes with unforgiving force, drowning each bite in syrup before shoveling it in. Since she wasn't going anywhere for a while, she'd wallow in misery and maple syrup.

"Coffee, Lucky?" Jessie lifted the pot, ready to pour.

He winked at her. "Only if it comes with a kiss, my golden-haired goddess of the griddle."

"In your dreams, flyboy." Jessie gave him a dubious look and handed him a mug of coffee.

Sadie admired the way these people got along. The pancakes were delicious, and the coffee was strong. She begrudgingly noted Kreston looked good, with snowflakes melting into his sandy brown hair and blue eyes catching hers. He'd pushed up his sweater sleeves despite the cold, and yes, okay—Aloha had a point about those arms.

*Stop,* she told herself. *Absolutely not. Forbidden fruit.*

No more evaluating Kreston's forearms. Or his eyes. Or the way he'd helped her in last night's storm without making her feel like she couldn't handle it. She definitely would *not* think about any of that.

"Mind if I sit?" asked Kreston, his hand on the back of the chair next to hers. His lips parted in a dazzling display of straight, white teeth.

"Sure. Take a load off." She found herself not wanting him to think less of her from yesterday's debacle.

*I'm not a bitch. Only stuck in an impossible situation out of my control.*

Kreston removed his coat and arranged it on the back of the chair, like he was attending a business meeting.

"How did you sleep?" he asked Sadie, as Jessie supplied him with a mug of coffee.

"Surprisingly well. The shower was a bit of a brown surprise, however," she said wryly.

"Have to let it run a spell for it to clear. The earthquake a while back shook the sediment loose inside the pipes." Tucker waved his hand back and forth.

"Meant to tell you about letting the water run a while." Kreston poured a heaping spoonful of white sugar and a generous glob of thick cream into his coffee.

Sadie hadn't seen anyone shovel mountains of real sugar and cream into their coffee since her dad did when she was little. Back then, no one blinked.

Kreston gave her a side-eye. "Something wrong?"

"I hope you know that's the kiss of death." She grimaced. "Haven't seen anyone avalanche a shit ton of sugar and heart-attack cream into coffee since the last century."

"You're that old, huh?" Kreston looked over his coffee as he sipped. "They no longer have sugar and cream in Seattle, the coffee mecca of the Pacific Northwest?"

This place really was a decade or two behind everywhere else.

*Yep, I've landed in a time warp.*

"Of course we do," sniffed Sadie. "But in this new millennium, we mostly use imitation sugar and nonfat creamer." She glanced around the table. "So, tell me, what does everyone do around here when it snows like this?"

"Right now, we're preparing for the holidays," explained Kreston. "Lucky and the boys plan to hang Christmas wreaths and cut trees for those who can't cut their own."

"In this wild-assed snowstorm?" Sadie's voice rose a notch. "You cut trees? You don't use artificial ones to conserve resources?"

Everyone at the table laughed. Kreston didn't answer. Instead, he sat there with a corner of his mouth lifted, running his finger around the rim of his coffee mug.

"What?" she quipped, piercing everyone with a stare. "What's so funny?"

"First, if we wait for the weather to clear in Alaska, nothing gets done," explained Lucky. "Second, have you seen how many trees we have in Alaska? Forests so dense the animals can barely squeeze their antlers and hineys between the spruce and birch."

"That's right," intoned Jessie, appearing at the table with one hand on her hip and the other lifting the pot of magical caffeine, fixer of the world. "It costs a fortune to ship a fake tree up here to the boonies. Besides, the state and feds like it when we thin the forest every year because cutting spruce reduces fuel for wildfires."

"How the heck do you haul the trees to town, then?" persisted Sadie.

Jessie smiled. "That's why God invented snowmachines."

Sadie held up her mug for a refill. "Why make fake snow when you have the real thing?"

Everyone chuckled and exchanged more knowing glances.

"Now what?" This was irritating, and Sadie was losing patience.

"Everyone Outside calls them snowmobiles." Kreston made a funny face and shivered. "Jeez, it slays me to say that evil word in Alaska. Feels like profanity."

The table burst out laughing. Everyone except Sadie, who didn't know whether to be mystified or annoyed. "Outside? Like out there?" She pointed to the window with her empty coffee mug.

More laughing at her expense. All right, this was officially getting old.

"Outside, meaning everywhere Outside of the state of Alaska."

"Oh." This weird place even had its own jargon. Well, so did Seattle: The Village, The Hill, The Market, and The Ave.

Jessie refilled Sadie's raised coffee mug. "Good girl. You know how to wake up with caffeine while it's still dark."

"Since I'm stuck here, I may as well overdose on caffeine." Sadie meant it as a joke, but it came out sounding like an insult.

Kreston set down his mug, and Sadie noticed him staring at her engagement ring.

"Don't worry, you won't be stuck for long. But you're welcome here just the same." He scooted out of his chair and swung his coat on. "If you'll excuse me, I have mail to deliver from yesterday's flight." He disappeared out of the Crooked Spoon, with Lucky on his heels.

"More pancakes, honey?" Jessie asked with a knowing smile. She lowered her reading glasses. "Hard not to notice the rock on your finger."

"Yes, to the pancakes. No, to the rock," Sadie tried to pull it off, but after drinking so much coffee, her finger had swelled. "Can't remove this stupid ring."

Jessie took the seat next to Tucker, who stayed quiet, meticulously sketching on a napkin. "Trouble down in paradise, I assume. Care to talk about it?"

"Nothing to say other than my ex-fiancé sent me a text intended for his mistress, or lover, or whatever you call a breaker-upper since we weren't married yet. We had plans to spend Christmas together at a resort in Talkeetna."

Jessie let out a long, descending whistle. "And now you're stuck here. Tough blow."

"Tell me about it," muttered Sadie, squirming in her chair. "I'll go crazy just sitting around. Without reliable internet or cell phone service, I can't work with my Seattle clients. I do public relations work."

Jessie rested her hand on Sadie's. "Tell you what. If you want to stay busy, you can help me out here at the restaurant. My server went to Fairbanks for the holidays. You could work off your hotel stay. I'll arrange it with Kreston if you're up for it."

"Kreston? Oh yeah, he's also the hotel manager." Sadie gave her a wary look. "I haven't waited tables since high school."

"Like riding a bike, easy peasy. We also serve breakfast all day here," said Jessie. "Also, I noticed our mayor couldn't take his eyes off you just now."

Tucker glanced up. "I'll second that."

Sadie shook her head in firm denial. "Why does everyone in this town play matchmaker for your mayor?"

Jessie shrugged. "Kreston has done a lot for people here. We just want him to be happy."

The way she said it tugged Sadie's heart, but she wasn't about to fall for the bachelor-in-paradise shtick. "I'm not the mail-order bride type. Just saying."

"Okay. So I imagined you checking out our mayor's fine physique. Got to get back to work. Let me know if you're up for helping." Jessie patted Sadie's hand, then stood. "You might want to get that ring off." She hurried off to the kitchen.

Sadie glanced at Tucker, still absorbed with his sketching. "I didn't mean to be rude about my remark about being stuck here." Her cheeks heated as she pushed bits of pancake around her plate. "What I meant to say was..." Her thoughts jumbled as she trailed off.

"No matter," Tucker slid his napkin toward her with a sketch of Sadie looking out the window. "Alaska has a way of giving people what they need, not what they think they want. Like sourdough pancakes. Or unexpected snowstorms."

His sketch was remarkably detailed. "Oh my gosh, this is superb, Tucker! You're a fantastic artist," gushed Sadie.

"Thank you, young lady. We know you don't want to be here, but we're proud of our little berg. I hope you can make mimosas out of orange juice." Tucker pushed himself to stand.

"Don't you mean make lemonade out of lemons?"

"Nope. We're into mimosas around here. A healthier beverage, by any standard." He winked, then shuffled out of the restaurant.

Sadie sat staring after him. Despite everything—despite Clayton and the storm and her ruined Christmas plans and being inconvenienced—she appreciated Tucker's act of kindness.

She studied the sketch he'd given her. He'd captured her disappointed expression. He's right—she should make the best of it. Maybe being stuck here wasn't the worst thing that could have happened.

Maybe it was only the second worst thing.

# Chapter 6

K*reston*

During the lunch hour, Kreston leaned against the doorframe of the Crooked Spoon, suppressing a laugh. Seattle's finest publicist served Mrs. Henderson's burger and fries directly into Mr. Henderson's lap. Jessie flitted by, whispering it was Sadie's third strikeout while serving lunch, including the decaf debacle that nearly started a riot with the noontime coffee crowd.

"I'm so sorry!" Sadie's voice sounded like she was barely holding it together. "Let me clean that up for you—"

"Table four's order is up!" Jessie called from the kitchen over the gentle strains of "Silent Night" from the cassette tape playing on an antique boombox on a corner shelf.

Kreston's mom had always kept the glove compartment of her Ford Mustang full of cassettes. He'd listened to Carole King's "Tapestry" and Linda Ronstadt's "Heart Like a Wheel" tapes until he knew every song by heart. Not his music choice, but he'd had no say on their long, lower-forty-eight road trips. His mom had passed away, so her cassette tapes provided some measure of comfort for him.

"Order up! It's getting cold," yelled Jessie.

"Coming!" Sadie spun around, nearly colliding with Lucky, who was showing his award-winning moose call to an unimpressed Ten Second Tess, whose attention focused on Sadie.

"Who are you? Are you from New York?" Tess demanded, adjusting her candy cane-striped scarf. "Our mayor is in love with you. He keeps staring at you." She pointed at him, then rushed off.

Kreston couldn't figure out how Ten Second Tess remembered he was the mayor, but she repeatedly asked Sadie who she was. At any rate, he ignored Tess's 'in love with you' comment and strode over to an empty table of dishes.

As Sadie scurried around, Kreston noted how fine she looked in the borrowed server apron. She wore it like armor, a defense in the fortress she'd built around herself. Dark red tendrils had escaped her ponytail, framing a face that appeared both delicate and strong.

Not that he noticed or anything.

"Order up!" Jessie hollered, emerging from the kitchen with gingerbread pancakes topped with red and green sprinkles. She paused beside Kreston, who was juggling an armload of plates, bowls, and silverware.

"Maybe instead of mooning at the hired help, you could actually help serve the food."

"What does it look like I'm doing?" Kreston spun around toward the kitchen when chaos erupted.

"Jessie, I'll serve those—" Sadie's offer ended in a yelp as she collided with Kreston. Dishes and silverware clattered to the wooden floor, while pancakes became airborne, and maple syrup splattered everywhere.

Sadie windmilled her arms as she skidded through the syrup in another pair of her non-sensible ankle boots with heels. Kreston instinctively reached out and caught her before she hit the floor. For a moment, they froze, with her back against his chest and his arms around her waist.

"Ice isn't the only slippery thing in Alaska." He was very much aware of how light she felt.

*Doesn't this woman ever eat?*

They both straightened, and Sadie pulled away. "Sorry, but I had everything under control."

"Just like you had the decaf situation under control?" He attempted a joke, but she wasn't smiling.

"How was I supposed to know Tucker would do that poetry-out-loud thing if he didn't get his regular coffee?" She threw her arms up, seemingly exasperated.

"Tucker is used to his routine, so when things go out of whack, he recites poetry. It's his coping mechanism." Kreston explained it as if teaching a science lesson.

From his corner table, Tucker looked up from his sketchpad. "The heart yearns for what it knows, like cream seeking its coffee, like sugar seeking its dissolution in the dark depths of meaning." He paused thoughtfully. "My ex-wife hated coffee. Should've seen that red flag."

Sadie stood looking at Tucker, bewildered. She didn't know what to say to that, so she turned to Kreston. "Don't you have mayoral duties to attend to or post office stuff to do?"

"Actually, I came to invite you to the Polar Creek holiday festival." Kreston motioned outside of the frosted windows, where vendors were setting up their canopy stalls, and business owners strung twinkling lights around their storefronts. The snow no longer blew sideways but fell straight down as if anvils weighted each snowflake.

"Every year we decorate the antler arch in the town square with red and green ribbons, and each window displays hand-carved, Alaskan ornaments. The town's founders started this tradition back in the 1940s." He glanced back at her. "You should join in the fun."

Sadie narrowed those remarkable amber eyes. "What kind of fun?"

"The usual. Outhouse races, sled dog races, and moose calling contests," replied Kreston. "And the ice fishing competition tomorrow where Tucker is judging, though he mostly recites poetry to the fish and grouses to them about his ex-wife."

Jessie moved through, stacking dishes and silverware on her large, round tray. "Tucker is quite the poet, actually. Last year, he wrote a sonnet comparing a salmon's love life to his marriage. Surprisingly moving."

"But salmon love lives end in tragedy," countered Sadie.

"Exactly," said Kreston, stroking his chin thoughtfully.

"Wait, back up. You said outhouse races?" Sadie wondered if she'd heard correctly.

"Team event with four people on a team," explained Kreston. "One is a helmeted rider sitting on a toilet seat with reading material and a roll of toilet paper. The other three push the toilet and rider on top of two sets of snow skis."

"Seriously? You've got to be kidding. That's ridiculous."

Kreston grinned at her horrified expression. "Come on, when was the last time you did anything completely ridiculous?"

"When I agreed to get on that plane with Lucky."

"See? You're on a roll!" he said with enthusiasm. "Besides, I need a fourth person for my team with Lucky, Jessie, and myself."

"Nah, I don't think so," Sadie pushed back.

"Free hot chocolate from Mrs. Larson's stand. She adds candy cane pieces." He tried luring her in.

"No."

He dangled another lure. "Bragging rights?"

"Are you kidding me?" She guffawed. "I'd be a laughingstock back home."

One last attempt. "Did I mention the toilet seat is heated?"

She broke out in a smile. "You're making that one up."

He waggled his brows. "Nuh-uh. Only one way to find out."

A half-hour later, Sadie was perched on a toilet seat, wearing Kreston's NASCAR helmet with the glittery red lightning bolts on either side.

"Thank God this toilet is unplumbed, but you lied about it being heated." She leaned over, eyeballing the toilet base bolted to a wooden pallet, and mounted on slippery skis that rested on the snow.

Kreston instructed Sadie to hold the roll of toilet paper high, like an Olympic torch. The rest of his team, including himself, Lucky, and Jessie, gripped the tow ropes as if their lives depended on it. Other teams took their positions on the starting line, including the rival team led by Hardware Bob, who'd won three years running.

"Can't believe I'm doing this. I've always wanted to sit on a throne," Sadie wisecracked.

"Befitting a queen," Kreston joked, organizing the team with their tow ropes.

Someone sang "Jingle Bells" with bathroom-themed lyrics and everyone hooted and hollered.

"Save your energy for waving the toilet paper," advised Lucky with an earnest face. "It's all about the presentation. Hardware Bob's team may have the faster toilet, but they lack our verve and enthusiasm."

Sadie's voice rose an octave. "Verve? How do I not fall off this thing?" She adjusted the moose antler headband Ten Second Tess had run up and placed over her helmet.

Kreston instructed, "Hang on tight. We don't want a repeat of what happened to Old Joe last year."

Sadie hesitated. "What happened to Old Joe?"

"Nobody knows, exactly," Kreston said with a somber expression. "But afterward, we called him One-Cheek Joe."

"Hey, Mayor Collins!" Hardware Bob called out. "Nice of you to enlist a neophyte to help you lose!"

"Ever hear of a dragon rider? This bonny badass is a toilet rider!" Lucky shot back, narrowing his eyes. "Be afraid, Bob. Be very afraid."

Ten Second Tess wandered over to Sadie, wearing mittens with bells. "Are you the mayor's girlfriend? Sorry you have to go to the bathroom in front of all these people. Nice antlers!"

Kreston opened his mouth to respond when the starting gun fired, and their makeshift chariot shot forward. Sadie's shriek trailed after them as they careened down Main Street, their crude little outhouse toilet sliding sideways on the packed snow.

"Lean into the turns!" panted Kreston, doing his best to tug them along.

"I'm on a flipping toilet!" Sadie shouted back. "There is no leaning!"

"Bob's gaining!" warned Lucky in a desperate battle cry.

"Wave the toilet paper like a cheerleader!" ordered Jessie, tugging her line for all she was worth.

"This isn't what I meant when I said I wanted a throne!" Sadie shouted as they slid from side to side. "I'd like to see Miss Manners handle *this* with grace." How their team managed to keep this ungodly contraption moving forward was a flipping miracle.

Kreston, Lucky, and Jessie tugged their ropes forward to control the side-to-side sliding. Before the race, they'd agreed to apply physics to their approach. Kreston glimpsed Sadie conducting the crowd with her toilet paper roll and tried not to laugh, since he was the muscle for this operation. The cheers grew louder, snowflakes swirling around them like confetti.

"Is that all you got, Seattle?" taunted Hardware Bob as his team pulled alongside.

"Who taught you to drive a toilet, a plumber's apprentice?" quipped Sadie.

Kreston smiled as he ran with the tow rope, liking how Sadie was getting into the spirit of this race. He'd sensed her competitive drive would fit nicely for this endeavor. He prided himself on his excellent judge of character.

Tucker yelled from the finish line, "The porcelain chariots speed across to destiny's drain!"

Oddly, they won. Sadie's toilet paper unrolled as she lifted it like a banner, brandishing it like one would a flag upon reaching the summit of Mount Everest.

Kreston stood back, breathing hard from the exertion. He'd finally beaten Hardware Bob, whose team had skidded into a snowbank, toilet seat spinning like a frisbee into the crowd. No one was hurt, but his team laughed so hard they couldn't get to their feet. Instead, they rolled around, cackling like hyenas.

"This was…" Sadie searched for words, shaking her head with flushed cheeks.

"Completely ridiculous?" supplied Kreston.

"Absolutely insane!" But she was grinning.

Kreston fished a long necklace from his pocket with a miniature toilet dangling from it, complete with a blue ribbon. He caught a whiff of Sadie's expensive perfume as he leaned in to slip it over her helmet. He inhaled again, loving the scent.

"As town mayor, I hereby deem you the winner! The rider gets the official prize and wears it for the rest of the festival. It's the ultimate honor to win the Outhouse Race." He was dead serious when he said it, but she laughed.

"What's next?" she asked, eyes sparkling. There was a slight paradigm shift in Sadie's attitude.

And he liked it.

# Chapter 7

*Kreston*

Next was a walking tour of Polar Creek's Christmas traditions. Kreston led Sadie past the snow-laden spruce to a display of ice sculptures carved with chainsaws. He pointed out a raven plucking a blueberry, a bear with paws in the air, and two leaping salmon, side by side, all carved from blocks of ice.

They passed several houses with the same plastic Santas and reindeer in the yards and on rooftops. Kreston explained how Home Depot had ordered too much holiday inventory in Anchorage last year, so the day after Christmas, Kreston bought two dozen at seventy-five percent off. He and Lucky flew to Anchorage and stuffed their planes with decorations and flew them back to Polar Creek.

Every door displayed a wreath made by a different family, and strings of lights created a canopy over the street, glowing softly under the snowfall, adding to the festive atmosphere. He was proud to show her his town.

Kreston saw an endearing side of Sadie, but he had to work like a dog to make her comfortable enough to show it. Each smile felt like a hard-won victory to gain her trust. Sadie reminded Kreston of trying to hold the Aurora Borealis in his hand, the way she dodged and weaved around his questions. When she let down her guard, she was impossible to pin down.

Her emotional defenses were as impenetrable as the Alaska Range, shielding her heart with an icy layer of permafrost.

He'd spent a great deal of time navigating treacherous weather and tricky landings—he knew patience and a cool head could overcome any obstacle. He considered it a challenge to see what lay beneath Sadie's protective layers, and there was no time like the present.

*What the heck? I'm a risk-taker.*

"I need to check on my dog team. Want to meet them? They're running in tomorrow's race." He motioned toward his truck, parked in its usual spot in front of the Polar Creek Hotel.

Surprisingly, Sadie lit up like a Christmas tree. "You have sled dogs?"

"Seven of 'em." They climbed into his truck, and he drove about a mile out of town. He pulled up in front of his spacious two-story log home.

"This is your home? It's beautiful," breathed Sadie, seriously checking it out. "Did you build this?"

"With the help of Polar Creek." He liked his easier rapport with Sadie, like finding solid ground after an earthquake.

"Come see my team. They're back here on the dog lot." As he expected, the cacophony of excited barking and howling of his seven Alaskan huskies welcomed them.

The dogs jumped down from the top of their doghouses, greeting them with enthusiastic yips and wagging tails. Sadie kneeled to accept their kisses. The largest male, with black-and-white facial markings, pushed to the front of the pack. He lifted a paw and howled hello.

"This is Denali," Kreston said fondly, scratching the dog's ears. "He's my new lead dog."

"What happened to your old lead dog?" asked Sadie when Denali extended his paw and covered her face with kisses.

"Long story," Kreston said dismissively, noting his dog cozying up to Sadie. "Look at that. Denali rarely warms up to strangers."

"Dogs seem to like me. I don't know why, I haven't had one since I was a kid." Sadie backed up, wiping her face with the back of her mitten.

Kreston was impressed at his normally aloof dog's enthusiastic greeting to the new woman in town. "I don't run them nearly as often as I should. Let's get you back to town. You must be tired after today."

"Yes, but a good tired, you know? I could use a good hot soak." She looked at him. "Are there any hot tubs in Polar Creek?"

"Funny you should ask. I have one on my back deck." He pointed to a tarped blob under the snow. "I'll fire it up for you one of these days." It was a good segue into a personal invitation, which made his heart skip with a morsel of hope.

"Think I'll take you up on that."

*Score one for the team.*

Kreston's face lit up, and he smiled to himself as they climbed into the truck for the drive back to town.

Jessie set down a plate of sugar cookies shaped like moose, caribou, and bush planes onto a table in the hotel lobby. She baked for anyone who happened in as her way of spreading holiday cheer; it had become her Christmas tradition. Things hadn't always been that way with Jessie. She was a broken soul when she'd arrived in Polar Creek years ago.

Kreston handed Sadie a caribou. "These are the best cookies you'll ever eat in your life."

Sadie bit into one and moaned. "Mm, so chewy. These are delicious!"

Jessie beamed. "So, where have you two been?"

"Took Sadie to see Denali and the team," said Kreston, trying to sound low key.

"Did he tell you about the accident?"

"Accident?" Sadie's eyes darted from Jessie to Kreston and back again.

Jessie looked at him. "Want me to tell her?"

Kreston shrugged. He didn't talk about it because it dredged up horrible memories he didn't care to remember.

Jessie's expression softened. "Two years ago, Kreston was training for the Iditarod. Had a real shot at it, too. Out on a trail just outside Denali Park, two snowmachines collided with the team. His lead dog was seriously hurt, and..." she trailed off.

Sadie's jaw dropped, waiting.

"I had to put him down," Kreston finished quietly. "His injuries were too much. I flew him to the Fairbanks pet emergency, but it was too late."

Sadie gave him an empathetic look. "So, you got a new lead dog?"

"A friend of mine in Talkeetna gave me a pup, and I named him Denali. Now I only mush for fun. No more distance training. Speaking of which..." He cleared his throat. "Want to ride with me in my sled tomorrow? It's only a loop through town, but a lot of fun if you've never been pulled by a sled dog team."

Sadie squealed. "Really? Yes!" The enthusiasm in her voice made him feel warm inside. She cleared her throat. "I mean, sure. If you want."

Outside, the festival was in full swing, with kids sledding down the hill behind the grocery store while their parents sampled Mrs. Larson's famous mulled cider.

The Gossip Trio teamed up to harmonize a sweet rendition of "White Christmas." Tall Martha played the harmonica, and her roommate, four-foot-tall Mini-Martha, was one heck of a fiddle player. Henrietta, the school librarian, was their next-door neighbor and knew her way around a guitar. She could play the introduction to Heart's "Crazy On You" like nobody's business. They called their group "The Polarizers."

Kreston explained all this to Sadie, then motioned at the door. "Want to go see what's going on before you head up to your room?"

Her gaze settled on him. "Sure, I suppose."

He opened the door, allowing her to step outside ahead of him. She nodded thanks, and they strolled along the wooden boardwalk from the hotel down to the general store, hearing the kids' laughter behind it, sledding on a man-made hill in the empty lot behind it.

They stopped to watch people stroll down the middle of the street under the canopy of twinkling lights. Kreston had loaned Sadie a pair of his extra-large warm gloves, and he noticed her hands swam in them. A strand of auburn hair had escaped Sadie's moose antler hat, and without thinking, he reached out to move it away from her face.

Their eyes met, and the snowflakes faded into a faint, ethereal mist. He was tempted to lean in for a kiss, but they were out here in front of the world. The town's mayor shouldn't be kissing random women in public—should he?

Lucky's voice rang out behind them. "Come practice moose calls at the Spoon! First round of hot chocolate and Bailey's is on me!"

"Poetry reading to follow," added Tucker, who'd shuffled up behind them. "I've written a sonnet about the holidays and plumbing maintenance, with sketches to go with it."

Sadie backed away to put distance between herself and Kreston, but he'd already caught her smile—softer than her usual sharp edges.

"I should—I have to help Jessie with the hot chocolate and cookies," she stammered.

*Wait a minute, is she blushing?*

"Try not to start any hot chocolate riots." Kreston observed her walking away, warmth waving through him that had nothing to do with the weather.

Something had shifted with her demeanor. For the first time since Sadie had blown into town, there hadn't been a cutting remark. The sled dogs seemed to have softened her a bit.

The Gossip Trio ambled toward him as he turned to get into his truck.

"We've been watching the two of you," gushed Henrietta, pushing her black cat-eye glasses higher onto her nose. "And we've decided you both make a cute couple."

Kreston hesitated before responding. Why fight City Hall? Besides, he was tuckered out from outhouse racing.

"Why thank you, ladies." He dipped a respectful nod, and they giggled as he climbed into his pickup and shut the door. When he started the engine, he lost himself in thought.

*Cute couple? Not happening.*

Like that would ever work out. Sadie is probably counting the minutes until she can fly back to Seattle. This isn't some sappy holiday movie where the big-city woman falls for the small-town guy.

Besides, he detested flannel shirts. Just because he lived in Alaska didn't mean he'd surrendered to lumberjack chic. He still possessed a scrap of dignity when it came to good old fashion sense. You can take the guy out of New York, but you can't always take the New York out of the guy. Well, at least not *all* of it.

*How else would I have known snow would ruin suede? Not that I would admit it to Seattle Barbie.*

As he drove home, he reflected on the day. Tomorrow would bring the sled dog races and more of Sadie's laughter. Or so he hoped. For the first time in a long time, he felt good.

The snow continued its steady determination to fall, adding another layer to Polar Creek's collection of holiday memories.

# Chapter 8

S*adie*
"More coffee, Tucker?" Sadie held up the pot, already knowing his answer after several days of serving at the Crooked Spoon.

"Do moose drop nuggets in the woods?" He pushed forward his mug—one he'd painted himself with a dancing moose wearing a tutu. "I must say, you're getting better at figuring out regular from decaf."

Sadie ignored what she hoped was a compliment. "The sonnet you recited about cream and sugar was actually pretty good." And she meant it.

"You should hear my haiku about hash browns." Tucker studied her over the rim of his cup. "You're settling in nicely. Despite yourself."

Sadie topped off his coffee. "Not settling. Just making the best of being stranded."

"That's what I said when I first came here. After the gallery fire." He traced the rim of his mug. "Did you know it wasn't even the fire that broke me? It was finding out why Myrtle did it."

"Your ex-wife?" Sadie slid into the chair across from him, now that the breakfast rush had ended.

"She thought I was having an affair with one of my students. Beautiful young thing, talented too. Painted Alaska like she could see right into its soul." He chuckled softly. "Myrtle never understood that not all passion is carnal. That young student reminded me of why I fell in love with art. I couldn't help that she was a female."

"What happened to your ex-wife?"

"Last I heard, she was shacked up in Anchorage with a used car salesman. She only got three months' probation and a fine for torching my art gallery." He shrugged. "I wound up with the better end of the deal. I got freedom and a new home, thanks to Lucky and Kreston, who brought me to Polar Creek. That mayor of ours has a gift for helping people."

"Like taking them in?" The domino effect Kreston Collins had on this town was slowly dawning on Sadie.

"Like seeing worth where others see wreckage." Tucker pulled out his ever-present sketch pad. "Now I sell my work in the hotel gift shop and split the proceeds with Kreston, though he never asks for a dime. Says my art belongs where people can appreciate it."

Before Sadie could respond, a whirlwind of activity burst through the door.

"Here comes the gossip factory," muttered Tucker. "Tall Martha, Mini-Martha, and Henrietta. They're trouble with a capital 'T.' Watch yourself." He got up and wandered off, leaving Sadie cornered like a reindeer in a hot tub.

"There you are!" the tall woman announced, her five-foot-eleven frame ducking slightly under the restaurant doorway. Obviously, Tall Martha.

The much shorter one must be Mini-Martha. She peeked around Tall Martha's elbow. "Don't scare the poor girl. We just want to welcome her properly."

"And get the scoop on the cheating ex," the third woman added, adjusting her black horn-rimmed glasses. "Hello, Sadie. I'm Henrietta. They call me Henrietta for short. Has anyone mentioned our mayor is single?"

"You're only the two-hundredth person who's mentioned it," Sadie replied dryly.

"From a technical standpoint, you're incorrect," Henrietta declared. "We only have a population of one hundred twelve."

"One hundred thirteen, now that you're here," piped up Mini-Martha, her rosy cheeks like two little apples on either side of her nose.

The three women grouped around her table like she was a celebrity.

Sadie couldn't suppress her smile. "Let me guess—Lucky told you about my ex?"

"Oh honey," Tall Martha leaned down and patted her hand. "Lucky only told one person, but the whole town knew before his plane landed."

"He's far more efficient than email." Mini-Martha and the other two nodded earnestly. "And more reliable than the internet. Speaking of reliable..." She waggled her eyebrows. "Kreston's quite the catch—"

"Alright, already!" Sadie's patience was wearing thin with this persistent matchmaking stuff.

"Did someone mention my dating status?" Kreston's voice came from behind the three women, causing them to jump. "Because I'm pretty sure that violates the town ordinance."

"Really?" asked Tall Martha. "There's an ordinance for your dating status?"

"Of course. I can make any ordinance I want. I'm the mayor." Kreston offered her a grin. "Unlike Alaska's boroughs and municipalities. That's the beauty of living here."

Henrietta nodded in agreement. "Polar Creek is a vast improvement over other places I've worked in rural Alaska. At least the kids here don't blow away during recess—unlike Kwigillingok and Tuntutuliak, where I was the school librarian."

Mini-Martha chimed in as all three headed for the door. "Just like it's true that certain mayors and Seattle visitors would make an adorable couple—"

"Goodbye, ladies!" interrupted Kreston, waving them out of the restaurant. He shook his head at Sadie. "People get cabin fever here in the winter, so they dwell on things like trying to get me married off. Just ignore them. They mean well." He dashed out of the restaurant and down the hall.

Curious, Sadie rose and followed him to the end of the hallway, where he ducked into a small room with a sign on the door: "Polar Creek Post Office." She leaned against the doorway, watching him stuff letters into a mail sack.

"You can't possibly have a town ordinance for your love life," she said, crossing her arms.

"No, but I should." He pressed his finger to his lips. "Shh, don't tell the Gossip Trio, though."

"Don't worry," she said with an exaggerated wink. "Your secret is safe with me."

"Want to help? Mrs. Henderson gets the large print catalogs." He didn't wait for an answer, only crammed letters into wooden mail slots lined up along the wall. "Tucker's art supplies go straight to the hotel, so stick those on that table there." He dipped his head toward it.

"Special delivery!" Ten Second Tess appeared in the doorway. "I have mail for Mayor Kreston!" She gave a blank look to Sadie. "Who are—?"

Sadie interrupted. "Sadie from Seattle."

"Oh, right, you're the mayor's mail-order bride!" chirped Tess.

Sadie gave Kreston a perplexed look, and he took it from there.

"She's not my mail-order bride." He handed Tess a bundle of letters. "Take these to Aloha right away before you forget. Go, go, go!" He shooed her out the door like a mischievous bear cub.

Sadie helped Kreston finish sorting the mail. She straightened with her hands on her hips, gazing at the multiple piles of letters, packages, and boxes.

"Most people come here to get their mail," explained Kreston. "Others can't always make it to town, so I deliver it to their homes."

"Next, I'm off to settle the ongoing snow storage dispute." He shouldered the mail bag and smiled. "Want to come along? Unless you have something better to do." He pulled on his jacket and offered her an extra one. "Here. Put this on."

She wrapped his oversized jacket around herself, inhaling its scent of pine and wood smoke. Kreston ushered her from his office, locked the door, and they stepped outside. Snowflakes caught Sadie's eyelashes, and her breaths were puffs of vapor as she followed him across the street to the mayor's office in the community center building.

Inside, the scent of coffee greeted them. Sadie paused at a large stuffed moose perched on a plant stand, holding a sign saying "Polar Creek Mayor."

"Last year's Christmas present from Lucky," Kreston explained, catching her stare.

The morning brought a steady parade of small-town problems, which Kreston handled with surprising grace. Three neighbors argued about where to store the white stuff, each refusing to pile it on their own property. Mrs. Henderson complained neighborhood kids had built their snowmen too close to her yard, scaring her cats. Kreston scribbled a note to tell the kids' parents to please relocate the snowman, snow-woman, and their snow-baby.

After Mrs. Henderson left, he confessed to Sadie, "I secretly think the snow baby is adorable, but you know how it is. Got to keep peace in the valley." He spread his arms in a what-can-you-do gesture.

A wide smile spread across Sadie's face. "Your corporate negotiation and problem-solving skills have come in handy."

Hardware Bob, practically blind without his glasses, showed up at the mayor's office, claiming one of Kreston's sled dogs had gotten loose and chased Bob's chickens and pet pigs around his homestead.

"Pretty sure that's not a husky, Bob," Kreston pointed out when Bob planted himself in front of his desk, holding up a photo of a confused wolf on his phone.

"But it's your lead dog, Mayor Collins. He responded to 'Denali' when I called him," argued Bob. "He even rolled over and played dead."

"So does Lucky when he's had too many hot-buttered rums. Wolves have been known to do that, too," explained Kreston. "I'll have Lucky take the wolf far from town and return him to the wild."

Speak of the devil. Lucky popped in, and Kreston asked him to fetch one of his dog kennels, lure the wolf inside with a moose steak, and take him to the far side of Grayling Lake. "And use your own moose meat. Don't raid my freezer like last time!" Kreston hollered after Lucky as he vanished out the door to run his errand with Hardware Bob on his heels.

"You'll be getting rid of Mayor Collins' best dog!" Bob yelled after Lucky as he toddled out the door.

Sadie silently watched the parade of complaints with amusement and fascination. She'd never been exposed to anything like this in the city. There was a lot to this mayor business. It wasn't easy keeping order in a small town. At least Kreston didn't hassle with bumper-to-bumper traffic and high crime. Not that she could tell, anyway.

Through it all, Kreston maintained his patience and kept his sense of humor, solving problems that would drive most people loony and they'd run screaming out the door. Sadie found herself in awe of how he blended common sense with creative solutions. He was nothing like the bureaucrats and polished executives she dealt with in Seattle—especially Clayton, her ex, with his careful image and calculated charm.

No, Kreston belonged in a category all his own. But maybe that was the problem—nobody could be this perfect. Didn't he have any flaws?

By the time they arrived at Kreston's dog yard to prepare for the sled dog sprint races, Sadie had gained a healthy respect for Kreston, the mayor. She observed how carefully he checked his dogs' paws and got them ready to load into the old pickup he used for hauling.

"You're good at all this," she commented.

"With the dogs?"

"No—yes, well, that too. I mean with people. The way you care. How you solve problems without making anyone feel small."

He looked up. "Easy to care when it matters."

And that was it, wasn't it? Everything here mattered. Every person, every problem, every solution. No spin required. A stark contrast to her world, where authenticity hid behind manufactured images, wrapped in layers of pretense.

"Ready to meet your racing team?" He gestured to the excited dogs. "Unless you're having second thoughts?"

She should be having second thoughts—about all of it. About how he handled broken lives with grace, solved disputes with humor, treated Tess with endless patience. About how different he was from the men she'd known in the lower forty-eight. And how none of it mattered because they lived in different worlds.

"I'm ready," she said, ignoring the voice in her head reminding her they had nothing in common except attraction. Well, maybe more than attraction, she begrudgingly told herself.

As she watched his gentle yet commanding interaction with his dogs, she realized he was completely in his element. For the first time since he'd opened the door to help her out of Lucky's plane, she wanted to know more about this person who appeared to have zero imperfections. She was determined to find one. Everyone had them. The only downside to looking for flaws—when you found them, it was hard to un-find them.

Forget it. She'd be out of here in a few days—as soon as the weather cleared.

"Want to give me a hand?" Kreston instructed her to open each of the seven wooden dog boxes. He then lifted each dog inside until all were safely loaded. "Take that end of the sled. Please," he added, lifting his end.

After they loaded the sled and Kreston secured it to the pickup, Sadie flung open the passenger door and hurled herself into the seat. "You need to install a step on this truck so people can get in easier," she huffed.

"That would ruin the fun of watching them climb in," he said laughingly, turning the ignition and driving along the snowy road toward town.

Sadie looked out the side window at the winter wonderland. She'd never been immersed in so much snow. Oddly, it made her feel insulated and protected, the way it muffled everything. She kind of liked it.

It hit her like a brick: she didn't know what she wanted out of life. She'd fallen into a job after college and worked her way up, jumping from one PR firm to another, until her current job was the pinnacle she'd always aimed for. And now that she'd reached it, she wasn't happy. Something was missing.

The universe had a funny sense of humor, orchestrating this inconvenience, showing her a slice of life she hadn't even known existed. She'd driven through small towns lots of times. But not one like this. Polar Creek was a weird, quirky town in a category all its own...and so were its residents. Especially this hotel manager, a.k.a. mayor, a.k.a. postmaster, and, oh yeah, bush pilot. She had yet to see him fly.

But she had a hunch he was really, really good at it.

# Chapter 9

*Kreston*

Kreston positioned his sled dog team at the starting line in front of the Polar Creek Hotel and the Community Center across the street. For the fiftieth time, he checked to make sure Sadie was warm and comfortable as she hunkered down inside the sled. He tucked her under the fox fur throw Jessie had made for him last Christmas.

"If you don't stop fussing over me, I'll tell Ten Second Tess to reorganize your clothes closet," Sadie said dryly.

He peered at her snow-speckled designer sunglasses he'd advised her to wear. No one likes flakes stinging their eyeballs. "Better not, or I'll tell Tess to unpack your humongous moving-truck-suitcases. Your undies would wind up in Jessie's freezer."

"Well, your tighty-whities would wind up in the ice maker," quipped Sadie.

"Ha, underwear on the rocks!" Chuckling, Kreston moved to his sled dogs and checked each one to make sure they were still wearing their dog booties. Jessie had made their booties red and green for the holiday races. Denali, of course, wore dark blue and gold booties as a nod to the colors of Alaska's state flag.

"Remember to hang on. My dogs are fast." He gave her a wink and a smile.

"This first race is just for fun since the dogs are pulling extra weight," Lucky explained as he helped Aloha settle into Jessie's sled. "In the official races, people don't ride in the sleds. Too much weight."

"Aloha! Welcome to the dog races!" announced Aloha from inside Jessie's sled. "Why do you think dogs have so many legs? Seems excessive."

Kreston hadn't thought about it like that.

Ten Second Tess appeared and tapped Sadie on the head. When she glanced up, Tess plunked a gargantuan white rabbit's foot onto Sadie's mitten. "Here's a snow hare's foot for good luck. What's your name?" Without waiting for an answer, she dashed off again.

"Snow hare?" Sadie gave Kreston a quizzical look.

"An Alaskan rabbit. Yeah, they're big, like everything else in Alaska." He strode off to check the dogs, making sure they weren't tangled in the gangline.

Sadie called out to him. "It takes Aloha and Tess to complete a thought, doesn't it? Good thing they hang out together."

Kreston chuckled as he walked back to the sled. "Aloha remembers, just not in the right order," explained Kreston. "It's like her brain bounces inside a Bingo ball machine and out pops a random memory, like a B-3 or O-64. Tess makes her feel better with her worse recall ability."

The starting line buzzed with excitement. Main Street had been transformed into a racing venue with residents on both sides of the street. Kreston had gotten up early to plow the race course with the wide plow on the front of his truck. The course began at the hotel, turned left to go around the town square's massive spruce tree, then looped through what Ten Second Tess always referred to as "the place where we put mail when it's lonely."

"The mailbox drop, Tess," Kreston had forever corrected her. He made one last check of Denali's harness, and his lead dog leaped into the air with so much excitement, all Sadie could see from her vantage point was a bouncing husky. The rest of Kreston's dogs yipped and barked, eager to run.

Once again, he checked on Sadie, wishing he could tamp down his anxiety and the pre-race flutters in his stomach.

"Truly, I'm fine," Sadie assured him as he stepped back to fiddle with his sled.

"He's always been this way," Lucky stood nearby and stage-whispered to Sadie, "Should've seen him back when he alphabetized his stock portfolios by how much anxiety they caused him."

"Put a lid on it, Lucky buddy. Too much information—" Kreston shook a gloved finger at his friend.

Sadie's shoulders shook with laughter, and his insides loosened.

Tucker appeared, a sketch pad in his hand. "Interesting thing about self-control," he mused, pencil flying across paper. "It's like trying to hold on to ice. The tighter you grip, the more it melts away."

"Point taken, Tuck, thanks." It always amazed Kreston how perceptive Tucker was. He took a deep breath, trying to relax. This would be the first time he'd raced since the accident.

"I must say, you're handling your pre-race jitters pretty well." Jessie checked the gangline that kept her dogs attached to each other and the sled.

Kreston figured he was an excellent actor if Jessie thought he had everything under control. He'd relax more once his dog team was on the move.

"Remember when Tucker made us sign liability waivers in triplicate?" teased Jessie.

"Still have mine framed in the bathroom," chirped Lucky with a grin. "Kreston's is in his outhouse."

Kreston's face heated. "All right, you guys, enough teasing. I need to focus."

Sadie twisted to look up at him. "They tease because they care. And because you're wound up tighter than a snowman's butt."

He hadn't realized his nervousness was that obvious. Maybe Sadie was more tuned into him than he thought.

"Don't know why I'm so hyped about this race," he grumbled. "Not like I've ever mushed before."

Sadie turned around. "I don't know squat about mushing, but I think these dogs know what they're doing. So go with the flow."

"Good thing the dogs know. Not sure about the human, though," jibed Lucky as he hovered near his wooden platform.

"Don't you have a plane to crash somewhere?" muttered Kreston.

"If this doggone storm would blow over." Lucky's voice changed to a note of encouragement. "Trust your dog team like they trust you. Show this town you're more than a mayor, a mailman, a bush pilot, and a hotelier."

Lucky glanced at Sadie inside the sled. "Did I leave anything out?"

To Kreston's surprise, she added, "The world's best problem solver."

"See, this lass is in your corner." Lucky elbowed Kreston, his Irish lilt kicking in. "Give 'em hell, laddie."

Sadie yelled her last-minute advice. "And don't sprain your brain overthinking it."

"Copy that," said Kreston, appreciating their encouragement.

The starting line filled with five teams, lined up one after the other. Kreston would be first off the line on account of him being the mayor and the one with the most mushing experience. Jessie's team was next as the second-most experienced musher; next was Hardware Bob with his mismatched huskies, then the Hendersons, and bringing up the rear were the two Marthas. Tall Martha mushed, while Mini-Martha rode in the sled basket.

"Each musher is timed, and the shortest time wins." Kreston aimed his explanation at Sadie.

"Gotcha," said Sadie. "Hey Lucky, why aren't you racing?" she hollered.

Lucky sauntered over. "I don't keep dogs. Don't have time for it when I'm mostly in the air. Besides, I enjoy helping Kreston take care of his." He turned and rested a hand on Kreston's shoulder. "You've got this, buddy. New team, new lead dog, new inspiration." He pointed his thumb at Sadie.

Kreston waved his buddy back to his platform. "Better get over to your post and start the race. You're officiating, remember? Got your starting flag?"

Lucky lifted an Alaska state flag. "Eight stars of gold on deck. And a field of blue ready for action!" He hollered through his bullhorn. "Mushers to the start line!"

Jessie yelled back, seemingly exasperated. "Jeez, Ohara, we're at the flipping start line already!"

As Lucky headed over to the portable wooden platform next to the spectators on the side of the street, Ten Second Tess ran up and stole the flag, waving it like a wild woman.

"Go, doggies, go!" she yelled for all she was worth.

Denali lurched forward, catching Kreston off guard, nearly yanking him off his sled runners. He yelled at Lucky as he sailed by. "Start the watch!"

Kreston's team flew forward, and he kicked the ground to give them momentum. His team sped by the frost-covered buildings, Christmas decorations, and the townspeople cheering from their porches.

"Woo Hoo!" yelled Sadie, twirling her mittened hand in the air. "This is amaze-balls!"

Kreston smiled at her enthusiasm. He figured she'd like this. Everyone did. When he had time in the summer, he gave Polar Creek's kids rides on his sled with wheels along the road to Grayling Lake.

"Lean left when Denali turns!" Kreston yelled to Sadie. Then he commanded his lead dog. "Haw! Haw! Turn left, Denali!"

His lead dog obeyed, gracefully turning in a wide left arc to go around the town square and the tall, full spruce decked out in Christmas lights. Halfway there. The course would bring them in a full circle back to the starting line.

Kreston finally relaxed, reminding himself of why he loved running dogs.

"Look at that!" Sadie pointed.

The official tree lighting ceremony was tonight, but Kreston had told Lucky to plug it in for the race. It was a beautiful, magical beacon shining through the falling snow.

As he shouted commands to his team, Kreston grinned, expertly steering his dogs back to the start-finish line in front of the Polar Creek Hotel. As he sped across the finish, Lucky lifted the stopwatch and clicked it.

Sadie shouted, "Yay, for Mayor Collins and Denali-And-The-Six!"

Ten Second Tess waved the oversized flag. "Okay! Get ready to start the race!" No one corrected her. They were too busy congratulating Kreston.

Jessie's team flew across the finish line, and everyone cheered again.

"Whoa!" she called out to her team.

Behind her, the rest of the teams arrived, and Lucky timed each one. Tucker recorded the times on his ever-present sketch pad. When everyone finished, Lucky and Tucker hunkered over the sketch pad in an animated discussion. Then Lucky lifted the big blue first-place ribbon he'd ordered online.

"Kreston takes it! He has the fastest time." Lucky grabbed the flag from Ten Second Tess and held it high. "Congratulations to Denali-And-The-Six!"

Sadie laughed. "I see my moniker caught on for your sled dog team." She extended her mittened hand for Kreston to help her out of the sled.

When he took it and tugged her to her feet, she stumbled into him with her hands on his chest. He was tempted to plant a kiss on her right then and there. Instead, he restrained himself. "The mark of a good publicist is creatively naming the contenders," he said, his breath coming out in fast frosty puffs.

Her face blanked, snowflakes catching auburn lashes and red lips needing to be kissed. For a moment, he forgot where he was until she backed up, chortling. "I'm good at what I do."

"You got that right," he breathed.

Tucker presented him with the blue ribbon and a plastic gold trophy of a golden retriever—the online store was fresh out of huskies—but Kreston didn't care. This win had bolstered his confidence, and he let out a happy, relieved sigh.

"You can add this to your resume." Sadie gave him a direct look. "Although something tells me your resume is more extensive than you've let on." She laughed, which altered his carefully ordered world.

"Time for the ice fishing tournament!" Lucky announced through his bullhorn to everyone milling about on the street. "Head on out to Grayling Lake, folks. Time to get your fish on!"

As the crowd dispersed and Sadie helped Kreston unharness the dogs and loaded them into their dog boxes on his pickup, Lucky swaggered over and sidled up to Sadie.

"A factoid you should know about our boy, Kreston, here," he said out the side of his mouth. "He's a control freak when it comes to his ice fishing holes. It has to be exactly to his specifications, meaning big enough for Alaska's largest grayling or Dolly Varden."

"Is that so?" said Sadie.

Kreston bumped Lucky's shoulder. "If you don't think big, you won't catch big."

"Same goes for humans, too." Lucky glanced at each of them and smiled.

Kreston broke the awkward moment. At least it was awkward for him, although he couldn't speak for Sadie.

"So, Sadie...have you ever gone ice fishing?" He waited. Sure enough, her stunned expression said everything. "Don't they do ice fishing down there in Seattle?"

She placed her mittened hands on her hips. "Of course there's ice fishing. We have lakes a few hours from town where people fish for perch and kokanee."

Kreston snorted. "Kokanee? Well, we have *real* salmon up here. But wait'll you taste an Arctic char."

She gave him a wide-eyed stare. "I presume that's a fish?"

He furrowed his brow, tapping his chin. "More like a lake monster. You know, like Nessie or one of those massive sturgeons?"

Her eyes popped off her face. "You have those here?"

"You'll see." He would enjoy every single minute of this.

# Chapter 10



Still flush with excitement from the sled dog race, Sadie hurried to her hotel room to pile on even warmer clothes, along with the pair of sensible boots without high heels Jessie had loaned her.

Kreston had offered to give her a ride out to Grayling Lake, so she hurried back downstairs. When she reached the lobby, Jessie was bundled up and heading for the door with Ten Second Tess and Aloha in tow.

"The check-in desk is closed, ma'am." Ten Second Tess pointed at a closed sign on the counter.

"Thank you, Tess!" replied Sadie without a second thought, realizing she'd fallen into the cadence of Polar Creek. It hit her like a lightning bolt: she was getting attached to these people.

*No, I can't do that! When I leave here, I won't be coming back.*

It was a cruel reality, but when this storm cleared, she'd be on the first flight out with Lucky. Or—would Kreston fly her out? No, it would have to be with Lucky. If she flew with Kreston, she might not get off his plane. She shoved the notion from her mind as she walked outside to Kreston's pickup. The huskies poked their heads through the round holes of their dog boxes, yipping a welcome as she approached.

Lucky swung open the passenger door. "You sit up front and talk to the driver while I get some shuteye." He winked at her like he was doing her a favor.

"Kreston, you need to carry a forklift to hoist people into this truck," she groused, grunting to lift her foot onto the impossibly elevated floorboard. "You need an altimeter for this thing. This is like boarding a semi."

"Semis are easier," Lucky said dryly.

"Haven't gotten around to ordering one." Kreston shifted the truck into reverse as Lucky heaved himself into the back seat and pulled the door shut.

The air was thick with snow falling when they arrived at Kreston's dog yard, though it had slowed somewhat. Sadie watched the two men work together to get the dog team situated. The way they moved between tasks and traded friendly jabs stirred something lonely inside her.

When was the last time she'd had a friendship like that? Her colleagues at work were pleasant enough, but her hectic schedule held everyone at arm's length. She missed having someone to share the everyday pieces of her life with—both the wonderful and the mundane.

Kreston moved to her with an ice chopper and a pooper-scooper. "Ever chisel doggy droppings from frozen snow for seven huskies? It's an amazingly satisfying experience." He held out each tool, grinning.

She looked at the tools, then at him. "No, but I have the feeling I'm about to learn."

Lucky called out, "There's an orange bucket next to Denali's doghouse. Have fun!"

Sadie stepped over to the line of doghouses and set to work chopping out doggie droppings, glad she couldn't smell them because they were frozen rock hard. She filled the bucket half full and presented it to Kreston, along with the tools.

"I love a woman who knows how to wield an ice chopper," he purred at her.

She laughed. "Is that how you Alaskan men size up the ladies? By how well we pick up doggie droppings?"

"You catch on quick, for a *cheechako*." Kreston grinned. "Ready for some ice fishing?"

"Sure, why not?" She stamped her feet to warm her toes.

Kreston didn't walk toward his truck. Instead, he headed to an outdoor garage and swung open the door.

"Ever ridden a snowmachine?" crowed Lucky. "Unlike those gutless lower forty-eight pieces of shi—"

"Ahem! Language, buddy." Kreston gave Lucky his evil-eye, then handed Sadie a pair of new foam ear plugs. "Stick these in first."

"Okay." She worked the soft orange foam inside her ears.

Kreston lowered a familiar helmet onto her head—the same badass helmet she wore in the outhouse race. She liked the red lightning bolts. Not her usual style, but it was liberating not to have anyone judging her.

She was sick and tired of being judged in her world. Another self-revelation. She couldn't care less how she looked at the moment. Come to think of it, she hadn't worn makeup since she'd arrived in Polar Creek. It seemed oddly out of place, so she hadn't bothered.

Kreston didn't seem the type who got wrapped around the axle about looks. Her ex sure had. All he'd cared about was showing her off as his trophy, always picky about her hairstyles, make-up, and clothing choices.

*I'm fed up with that, too.*

Maybe it was a good thing fate had intervened with Clayton, sending her the onerous text. She wondered if he'd tried calling or texting her. Surely, he'd noticed by now, she hadn't returned to Seattle.

Lucky swung a leg over his Arctic Cat, as did Kreston, who motioned her to sit behind him. "Hang onto my waist," he ordered.

Even with the warm layers and thick jacket, she enjoyed reaching around his waist and hanging onto him. The back of his forest-green parka smelled good to her. A combination of dogs, winter air, and a hint of the potpourri Aloha kept in bowls around the hotel lobby. She liked it.

Kreston popped earplugs into his ears, then tugged on his helmet. He and Lucky started the engines, and they were off, speeding down the snowy road from Kreston's place to Grayling Lake. She loved how he maneuvered his snowmachine around the curves and how the powder trailed after them. The only downside was the ride ended too soon.

Kreston slowed to ease his Arctic Cat onto the lake ice before skittering out to the ice fishing shacks in the center, where he cut the engine. "Welcome to Polar Creek's holiday ice fishing tournament."

"Are you sure it's safe out here?" Sadie eyed the snow-covered ice, casting furtive glances around her. The falling snow had lessened for a spell.

"We wouldn't be out here if it wasn't," Kreston assured her.

She glanced up at a sight that had her mouth agape, tugging Kreston's sleeve. "Is that Denali Mountain through those snowflakes?"

He lowered his sunglasses and teased, "Does a salmon swim upstream?"

"All right, smarty pants." She fumbled her phone from her pocket and powered it on to take a photo. "I can't believe how high it is!"

"Get your fill, because it's a rare thing when she's out."

Sadie held up her phone. "You referred to Denali Mountain as a female. I like that." She gave him a demure smile.

Lucky pulled up on his snowmachine, his grin visible above his frosted red beard.

"What are you so happy about?" Kreston removed his helmet and shook his hair, like a hot guy in a shampoo commercial, causing Sadie's breath to hitch. "You look like Tess when she discovers another bizarre way to organize soap."

"Oh, nothing," shrugged Lucky. "Just wondering how you two will get along in a two-person shack for hours on end."

Kreston made a face at him. "And what makes you think it will take hours? I plan to catch the winning fish in the first hour. No, make that the first half hour!"

"You seriously have control over that?" asked Sadie, not believing a single word.

"You don't think I'll do it?" Kreston gave her a triple-dog-dare look. "Care to bet on it?"

Sadie wasn't one to back down from a challenge. "I'll do you one better. I'll bet you I'll be the one who catches the winning fish in the first half hour!"

Kreston guffawed and pointed at her. "You got yourself a bet. What are you betting?"

Sadie thought for a minute. "If I catch the winning fish in the first thirty minutes, you will cook my fish for dinner tomorrow night at the Crooked Spoon *and* serve it to the customers. And while everyone enjoys my winning fish, you'll serenade them with a song of my choosing, wearing my moose antler hat."

His jaw dropped. "You can't be serious."

She folded her arms. "Dead. Serious. Take it or leave it."

"You drive a hard bargain, Seattle. And if I win?"

"I do the same."

"Agreed. With one slight change. You'll sing 'The Alaska Flag Song' while waving the flag."

"Interesting choice. But okay, agreed." She extended her hand. "Shake on it."

He shook it just as Tucker moseyed up with a clipboard. "As Mayor, you must sign this roster of ice-fishing teams over at my truck. It's an official document. Don't want to get it wet." He blinked snowflakes from his eyelashes.

Kreston and Lucky moseyed off with Tucker, laughing and talking, with Lucky's arm around Kreston's shoulder. He punched Kreston's arm and pulled away, laughing. Sadie wished she could hear what they were saying.

Jessie appeared next to her. "I put Tess and Aloha to work decorating the ice shacks."

"They're doing a wonderful job. It looks like a Hobbit holiday village on ice," said Sadie, nodding.

The tiny shacks dotting the frozen lake were each decorated with haphazard strings of battery-powered twinkling lights.

Sadie squinted. "Those wreaths look familiar. Are they made with red and green hotel towels?"

"I'm afraid so," said Jessie. "Tess and Aloha's designs."

"There's something I've been curious about. Why does Lucky seem connected to Kreston at the hip? Does Lucky work for him?"

"Kreston and Lucky worked out a barter system. It's a common thing we do in Alaska." Jessie pressed a cardboard cup of hot chocolate into Sadie's hands. "Lucky helps with Kreston's dogs, and whatever odd jobs crop up, and Kreston helps Lucky with plane mechanics. They don't keep track, but it always seems to balance. Kind of like how you and Kreston balance each other out." She stated it as fact, sending a shock wave through Sadie.

"How so?" she stammered.

"Honey, the man has always kept neat, organized offices at the hotel and the mayor's office," said Jessie. "But since you arrived? His office looks like the Grinch went to work on it."

"Oh." Sadie wasn't sure what to make of it, but she understood what Jessie meant about balance.

"Opposites attract, you know. Just saying." Jessie pointed out. "I better go see what Tess is up to. Keeping track of that girl is like trying to nail Jell-O to a glacier. See you later." Jessie moved off, leaving Sadie to her own devices.

Sadie hadn't considered that angle. From the moment she'd stepped off Lucky's plane, the whole town had been trying to push her and Kreston together. She'd resisted their matchmaking attempts, brushing off their comments and hints. After all, what was the point of developing feelings for someone when she'd be leaving soon?

And a quick fling wasn't her style. Unlike some women she knew who could separate emotions from physical attraction, she couldn't just shelve her feelings for casual sex.

That wasn't how she rolled.

Kreston strode over. "Snow has let up a bit. Weather forecast says it'll taper off tomorrow." He let it hang there, and she let it.

*I guess it's time to leave this godforsaken place.*

# Chapter 11



**S**adie

She wasn't ready to leave Polar Creek yet; she needed more time to make good on her bet with Kreston.

Lucky came up behind them. "So, you replaced me as your fish buddy?" he teased.

"I'm showing Sadie the ropes," said Kreston. "There's only room for two, as you know."

"Fine. I know when I'm not wanted." Lucky pretended it hurt his feelings.

Kreston gave him a dour look. "You're only twenty feet away in the next shack. Ten Second Tess will be your fish buddy if you don't mind her forgetting why she's in there with you."

"Oh, no, you don't," countered Jessie, walking up to them. "I have a hard enough time keeping track of that girl. I don't want to go pounding on ice fishing shacks looking for her. Besides, it would scare the fish away and tick everyone off."

"Let's get started, folks." Kreston motioned Sadie to follow him to a shack in the middle. He opened the rickety door. "Welcome to Collin's Fish House, where we sit in a tiny box, freezing our buns off, waiting for fish. When the aliens land and abduct us, they'll be mystified. Have a seat, Miss Sadie." He swept his arm in a come-on-in gesture.

The six-by-six shack was surprisingly cozy, with a portable battery-operated heater to warm the space enough to shed their jackets. Sadie sat on one of the two folding chairs, watching Kreston methodically prepare the 24-inch diameter fishing hole with the same precision she'd observed when he organized other tasks.

Kreston baited two hooks and handed Sadie a fishing rod. "When you get a strike, let the fish take the hook. If you yank it, you'll lose the fish. Got it?"

Sadie made a face. "I've fished, you know. We have fish in Seattle."

He lowered his chin and looked at her. "Let me guess. You get yours at Pike's Market."

Her eyes flicked to his, and she narrowed them. "How did you know that?"

He ignored her question with a quiet smile and powered up his phone. "Alarm goes off in thirty minutes."

"Let's get this fish bet started, then." She moved her rod up and down to lure in an unsuspecting fish. "Tell me something. I want to know what you did before you came to Polar Creek. Where are you from originally?" Sadie glanced up to see a shift in Kreston.

He stiffened, staring into the dark water in the ice hole. "Miami Beach."

She spluttered. "Excuse me? You're from...Florida?"

Kreston raised and lowered his fishing rod. "Left at eighteen. Went to Harvard, got a degree in investment banking, then got offered a job in New York City. Lived the American dream, complete with a house in the Hamptons and a smart, attractive woman who wanted to marry me. Then the meteoric rise and the crash and burn when the bottom fell out of the stock market." He went on to explain the gory details.

Sadie couldn't believe what she was hearing. This was the absolute last thing she expected him to say. He talked about the market crash like someone describing a car accident in slow motion, each detail crystal clear as if it happened yesterday.

"I was focused on success, wanted it at any cost. It's what my parents wanted and what everyone else told me I wanted." Kreston stared at the fishing hole as if gazing into the past. "I was hellbent on the perfect life. I didn't realize how empty it was until the dominoes fell and I lost everything...even the girl."

Sadie was on the edge of her seat, mesmerized. "What happened next?"

"Lucky happened." He chuckled. "He found me in an Irish pub in Manhattan, drowning in cheap scotch and self-pity. He was planning to fly to Alaska and invited me to go along. I was drunk enough to think getting a pilot's license was the next logical thing."

"You learned to fly just to come to Alaska?"

"Wanted to earn a living as a bush pilot." He chuckled. "Lucky showed me there was more to life than spreadsheets and stock options. Sometimes the best things happen when your carefully planned life falls apart."

"Boy, isn't that the truth?" Tears prickled Sadie's eyes, understanding all too well.

"It's no secret why you wound up here in Polar Creek," he drawled. "Lucky told me your ex cheated on you?" He reeled in his bait, checked it, then let out his line again.

"Yeah." She told him the whole story—about Clayton's betrayal with the misdirected text, her disillusionment with her job, and the hollow victory of reaching the top.

"I wanted to help people create positive public images," she confessed, her voice thick. "Now, my job has devolved into hiding their embarrassing mistakes. And I'm good at it. Really good. But now? When I look in the mirror, I don't recognize myself." A tear fell on her cheek.

"Hey," Kreston's voice was soft. "You're being too hard on yourself. It sounds like you needed this break." He offered her a tissue, and she knew by his faint smile he understood.

She dabbed at her eyes, grateful for his support. It helped to know he'd survived the same jaded corporate wasteland she'd been drowning in.

"Do you have a girlfriend?"

He thought for a minute. "Hm, girlfriends. Not that I can think of. I've dated a few, but none of them panned out to be anything serious. There was one woman named Rochelle I dated for the better part of four months, but she got a job offer and left Polar Creek."

"Did she break your heart?" asked Sadie.

He guffawed. "Not really. We were more like good friends than anything. I wasn't gutted or anything when she left."

Sadie's fishing line suddenly went taut, then her rod jerked like someone was under the ice, yanking it.

"Fish on!" Kreston was instantly in motion. "Reel it in—steady—easy does it—"

Sadie jerked to stand, knocking over her chair. She gripped the rod with her left hand and reeled with her right.

Kreston peered into the hole. "I see him! He's a big one!" He reached for a net. "You must lift the fish out before I can net it."

Sadie lifted the line with her hand, and an Arctic char burst from the hole like a silver missile. Sadie jumped back and screamed as the fish flipped off the hook. Slushy water splashed them as the massive fish flopped around the shack like it was searching for the door.

Kreston grabbed a baseball bat and shouted, "Grab hold of it so I can smack it on the head!"

"You can't beat a fish with a freaking baseball bat! That's animal cruelty!" Sadie flailed around, trying to catch the wildly flopping fish.

He shot her an astonished look. "How do you expect to kill it?"

"Doesn't it just lay there and die?" She gave him an exasperated shrug.

Kreston rolled his eyes, then hopped around with the bat like he was dancing on home plate at Wrigley Field. His feet slipped from under him, and down he went, sprawling on the ice, still gripping the bat.

The slimy fish executed a backflip and sailed across the shack. Sadie tossed her jacket over the hole in case the little bugger made a break for freedom. Only he wasn't so little. "Oh, no you don't, Bubbles McGraw!"

Kreston scrambled to his feet. He made a grab for the elusive fish but slid straight into the wall instead. He spun around to see the wild-assed fish knock over their bait bucket, sending dead minnows skidding across the ice like tiny silver pucks.

"You suck at catching fish!" Giving chase, Sadie's boots skidded on the bait, and she crashed into Kreston's chest like a defensive tackle. His arms encircled her, and they froze, their lips inches apart.

"You should play for the Seattle Sea Hawks," he murmured.

"I could use a new job." She gripped his sweater, staring into his baby blues.

He leaned in close until there was barely a centimeter between their lips. He slid one hand into her hair, the other firmly gripping her waist.

Sadie's heart already raced from chasing the fish, and now it cruised up to light speed. She closed her eyes, anticipating a kiss to rock her world.

Tucker burst through the door. "Heard hollering and screaming. Did you catch a fish?" With a hung jaw, he took in their intimate stance, the scattered bait, and the train wreck of an ice shack. His gaze rested on the Arctic char, which had given up the fight and lay defeated in the corner.

Lucky peeked in. "At least you have the fish on ice." He glanced around. "Did a sharknado blow through here? What the heck were you two doing?"

Kreston pulled off his glove and bent to pick the fish, holding it up by the gills. "We've got ourselves a winner, unless someone else caught a bigger fish."

The whole ice fishing contingent had gathered, peeking in. Tucker weaseled his way to the front. He squinted one eye, making an 'L' with his thumb and forefinger to do an air measure. "It's a winner. You won by default. No one else caught a fish."

"Let's put Christmas lights on that lady's fish. What's her name?" Ten Second Tess held up a blinking string.

"My name is Sadie, and I caught the biggest fish!" she shouted from inside the shack.

"Step outside for our winner's trophy!" Tucker waved them out.

When Kreston and Sadie stepped outside, Tucker presented her with a plastic bass wearing a Santa hat that flopped its tail on a wooden plaque and lifted its head to sing "Santa Baby" when you squeezed its nose. In reality, it was Eartha Kitt's voice, but the fish lip-synched it perfectly.

"We had a proper trophy, but a grizzly stole it last year and ate it," explained Jessie, sipping a hot toddy from a steaming mug. "This was all we could find on the Trophies-R-Us website."

"Want to know the best part?" chirped Sadie. "I won a bet with Kreston! He has to cook my fish at the Crooked Spoon and serve it to customers for dinner tomorrow. And the best part?"

Everyone looked at her expectantly.

"Kreston must serenade the dinner crowd with a song of my choice!" Sadie squeezed the bass nose, and the fish sang its own "Santa Baby" congratulations.

"Ha ha, funny," said Kreston, but Sadie saw his eyes sparkle.

Whoops and hollers broke out with applause.

"Congratulations, Sadie! We'll all show up for dinner with bells on," hollered Lucky. "Hey Tucker, it's time for an ode to fishing poem."

"Don't you dare, or we'll never get back to town," warned Kreston.

Undeterred, Tucker launched into a verse. "There once was a fish in a shack, whose catching required quite a knack. Two people went in, and came out with a grin, and a fish that got them on track!"

Everyone laughed and applauded while Tucker took a bow. "Now go do your mayor stuff." He shooed Kreston off like a stray mutt.

"Remind me to get new friends," joked Kreston as he took Sadie's hand and led her to his snowmachine for the ride back to town. As they trudged through the drifts, she squeezed the fish nose, and strains of "Santa Baby" echoed across the lake.

Kreston twisted to look at her as they climbed onto his snowmachine. "We have a holiday party tomorrow night. I'm officially inviting you to go."

"Like on a date?" Her little heart went pitty-pat.

"You want it to be a date?"

"If you want it to be a date."

"Okay then. It's a date."

Sadie caught his eye and smiled as they put on their helmets. Losing control of a wild-assed flopping fish situation wasn't the worst thing that could have happened. Maybe it was exactly what a person needed...like getting stranded in Polar Creek.

The puzzle pieces were falling into place for her.

The weird part was, it made perfect sense.

# Chapter 12

K*reston*

The next morning dawned to find Kreston at his desk in the mayor's office, staring at a mountain of paperwork. Each spreadsheet tracked another crisis caused by the storm. His office closed in on him, as if his responsibilities were physically taking up space, crowding him like unwanted house guests.

"No mail delivery for nearly a week, and tomorrow is Christmas Eve," he muttered, updating his ever-growing list. "Generator at the hotel needs checking. Henrietta's pipes froze. The school roof is—"

"—about to collapse under your self-imposed burdens?" Jessie appeared in his doorway, holding coffee and cinnamon rolls. She had the look—the one that meant he wasn't getting out of this conversation, no matter how many excuses he came up with to dodge it.

"I didn't ask for breakfast delivery."

"That's why you need it. You refuse to ask for help even when you're drowning." She set the food down on his worn oak desk and settled into the chair across from him.

"Remember, five years ago when you refused to call for help when I found you crying with a black eye in the Spenard Roadhouse restaurant in Anchorage?" he countered.

"That was different. I was on the run and couldn't tell anyone."

"If you recall, I didn't pummel you with questions," he reminded her. "I just listened when you asked me to please help you disappear and start over."

She pushed a cinnamon roll toward him. "And you moved mountains to create a perfect paper trail for 'Jessie Thompson,' complete with a failed business venture so my abusive husband wouldn't find me."

He bit into a cinnamon roll. "I did what anyone else would do, given the situation."

"No. You did what *you* always do. You saw me drowning and threw me a lifeline, despite you barely being able to keep your own head above water." She fixed him with a stare. "It's high time you let someone throw *you* a lifeline for a change."

"I'm not drowning," he insisted, ignoring the pain poking at his chest. He knew what she was getting around to saying, and he shifted in his chair.

"Really? Because this morning your office was mysteriously organized, and yesterday you reorganized the emergency supplies in the hotel after Tess stashed them in the kitchen freezer."

"I always do that," he countered. "We can't store emergency supplies in the freezer."

"Kreston, come on." Her voice softened. "Talk to me. What's really bothering you?"

Words had a way of coming out easier with Jessie. She'd seen him at his worst, fresh off his Wall Street debacle, trying to figure out which end of a mop to use while wearing designer shoes instead of insulated boots.

"She's going to leave, Jessie." He knew he sounded pathetic but couldn't help it. "Once the weather clears, Sadie will return to her life in Seattle. And I'll still be here, making sure Ten Second Tess doesn't reorganize the supply closet, flip brooms upside down, or stuff toilet paper inside the mop bucket."

"Remember when I left my old life in the dust? The one with the country club membership and the perfect society marriage that came with perfect society bruises?" Jessie reminded him.

He winced. "What does that have to do with this?"

"I'm making a point," she said firmly. "You help everyone else but yourself."

"Oh, when have I done that?" He snorted in a contradictory manner.

Jessie threw up her hands in frustration. "Okay, Clueless Wonder, how about when Lucky's family disowned him for choosing bush planes over banking, and you left your whole life behind to fly with him to Alaska? You arrived in Polar Creek with nothing but a broken Rolex and a Harvard degree, and you refused to ask for help. How about when you brought Tucker here after the fire? Not to mention Aloha and Ten Second Tess? Hell, you've rescued half the people in this town!"

She sat back and heaved out an exasperated sigh. "It's high time you think of yourself first for once."

He didn't know what to say. Sure, he'd done those things, but it was his way of seeking redemption for himself and his failed life. Helping these people had given him a renewed sense of purpose instead of feeling like a battle-weary loser of the American dream.

"The thing is, I don't want her to leave, but I also don't want her to stay," he forced out. "Getting involved again scares the shit out of me."

"It scares the shit out of all of us," admonished Jessie. "Look, you can't have it both ways. Come on, Kreston, man up! Pull up those tighty-whities and face the fact you have feelings for Sadie Foster."

"And then what? She has a life back in Seattle, and I sure as shit don't want to move back to the lower forty-eight," he said defensively.

"All I can say is, you'd have to be blind not see the change in both of you when you're together. I'll bet she's been more herself here than she ever was in Seattle."

He shook his head. "Jessie, it's an impossible situation."

"Don't give me that crock—make it possible! Was it possible for a high-society wife to become a small-town cook? Or for a Wall Street hotshot to find happiness running a town and a hotel in nowhere, Alaska?"

"So, what do you expect me to do?" he asked quietly.

"I'll give it to you straight." Jessie reached across to squeeze his hand. "The universe has plunked what could be the gift of a lifetime for you in Polar Creek. I think it would be a huge mistake for you to allow this wonderful gift to fly away."

Suddenly, Ten Second Tess appeared in his office doorway with a concerned, wide-eyed expression. "Someone stole the cinnamon rolls!"

"No one stole them, Tess." Kreston pointed at them. "Here they are. Jessie brought them over."

"Oh! Never mind, then." Before he could respond, Tess vanished from his office just as suddenly as she'd entered.

"I can't figure how she remembers our names but not how to organize a closet." Kreston shook his head. "Should she be out wandering around?"

"She'll be fine. I'd better get back to the Crooked Spoon." Jessie stood and tapped his desk. "Think about what I said. That's an order."

"I better get over to the hotel, too. I'm on the hook to grill an Arctic char for dinner." He scratched his nose. "And apparently, I have to sing a song. I guess you'll have to set up your karaoke machine in the restaurant."

"You? Sing?" Jessie chuckled. "Oh, right. The fish bet. You have the afternoon to prepare. And don't forget the holiday party tonight."

"Right. I brought my party clothes with me this morning. Won't have time to go home and change. Wait a second, and I'll walk over with you." Kreston grabbed his jacket from its coat hook, and they stepped out of his office and across the street to the hotel, where he got to work reviewing supply orders. He smiled at the regulars as they gathered in the hotel lobby for their daily afternoon confab.

He was walking out of the hotel office to chat with Aloha at the check-in desk when the lobby door burst open. Sadie staggered in, holding a limp but semi-conscious Ten Second Tess in her arms.

"What the—" he started. "What happened?"

"Found her in the snow on the school playground. I think she's hypothermic." Sadie's voice cracked with urgency.

The lobby erupted into chaos as people rushed over.

"Get some blankets and a bowl of hot soup!" shouted Lucky.

"Pour her a cup of tea!" Tucker called out.

"Someone call a doctor!" hollered Aloha, setting down her deck of cards.

"Hot water bottles!" the Gossip Trio chimed in.

Sadie's voice sliced through the panic like a machete. "Everyone, calm down!"

Kreston felt his insides shift. He liked it when people took charge of a situation. Thankfully, it was someone else for a change.

"Kreston, carry Tess up to my room," ordered Sadie, and instructed everyone else. "Lucky, find extra blankets. Tucker, tell Jessie to bring up a pot of tea. Aloha, call..." she paused and looked at Kreston. "Who should she call? Do you have 9-1-1? Please say there's a doctor in town."

"Aloha, use the landline to call Hardware Bob's wife. Tell her to please get here as soon as possible," he ordered, and Aloha headed for the phone.

"Janet is Polar Creek's nurse practitioner," Kreston explained, lifting Tess from Sadie's arms and easily climbing the stairs.

"Hope she gets here fast." Sadie trailed behind as they rushed upstairs to her hotel room, where Kreston gently laid Tess on the bed.

"She's shivering," noted Sadie. "Body heat is our best option to warm her. Please go downstairs and tell Jessie I need her help up here immediately."

"Will do." Kreston sprinted down the stairs, his mind racing.

What had Sadie been doing out in the storm? Had she gone looking for Tess and somehow tracked her through the snowstorm? Sadie not only found Tess, she'd carried her back and took charge of the situation while everyone else panicked. She saw what needed doing and did it.

Kreston had been so wrapped up in his own fears, he'd missed the obvious: Sadie didn't belong in Seattle.

*She's like the rest of us—she belongs here.*

According to Jessie, the life we think we want isn't always the one we need. He knew what he had to do, and he would make it happen tonight at the holiday party.

Hopefully, Ten Second Tess would be okay with Sadie and the entire town looking after her. But Kreston had a feeling he wouldn't be. Not with Sadie melting his carefully constructed walls of defense, one brick at a time.

He'd run out of excuses. He'd pull up his big boy whitey-tighties and tell a certain city slicker from Seattle how he felt about her.

And it scared the holy living daylights out of him.

# Chapter 13



Sadie tugged off Tess's boots and removed her wet clothes. She never imagined her crisis management skills would translate to a hypothermia emergency. But a crisis was a crisis, whether in a Seattle conference room or an Alaskan hotel room in the middle of nowhere.

When Jessie showed up at her hotel room, Sadie didn't mince words. "Direct skin-to-skin contact works fastest to raise core temperature. Everything else can wait." She glimpsed Kreston in the hallway. "Don't come in for a while. Thanks, Kreston."

He nodded. She closed the door and stripped down to her underwear.

"This is all my fault. She came to the Mayor's office earlier, and I just blew her off," lamented Jessie, shaking her head as she toweled Tess dry, briskly rubbing her arms and legs.

"No time for that. Get undressed," instructed Sadie.

Tess moaned softly, and Sadie put her face next to hers. "Tess, Jessie and I are going to warm you up by lying next to you." She hoped Tess would understand.

They worked quickly. Tess's skin was frighteningly cold, her lips tinged blue. The women positioned themselves on either side of her, pressing close to warm Tess with their body heat. They piled blankets over all three of them.

"Good thing you found her when you did," Jessie murmured, rubbing Tess's arms briskly. "She apparently forgot she needs to wear coats in the wintertime."

Janet arrived minutes later and came through the door with her medical kit and a healthy supply of hot water bottles. She moved with the efficient certainty of someone used to these kinds of emergencies.

"Textbook treatment, good job." Janet approved, checking Tess's vitals. "Bilateral body heat on both sides is exactly what she needs. Keep it up."

While Janet monitored Tess's pulse and breathing, Sadie massaged Tess's limbs to improve circulation. Jessie stayed pressed against Tess, sharing body heat with her core. The minutes crawled by like hours.

At last Janet announced, "Her temperature is rising. She's out of danger."

The women sighed with relief and eased away from the bed while Janet tended to Tess.

As if on cue, Tess's eyes fluttered open. "Where am I? Hi Jessie. Who are you?" She gave Sadie an accusing stare, her eyes darting between the three women. "Why are you two naked?"

Sadie yanked a UW sweatshirt from her bag, and Janet and Jessie helped Tess put it on.

"Ooh, this is soft. I'm so tired," yawned Tess, lying back down.

"Come on, honey," Jessie was already helping her up and out of bed. "Let's get food in your belly. I have chili and cornbread on the stove downstairs."

Sadie tossed Jessie a pair of leggings to help Tess dress the rest of the way. Jessie escorted Tess out of Sadie's room and into the hallway.

"Thanks so much, Sadie. If you hadn't found her..." Jessie choked up.

"But I did," Sadie quickly assured her. "It's okay now, Jessie. Don't play the blame game."

"Jessie!" Kreston's voice rang out from down the hallway. "How is she?"

"Much better," said Jessie. "I'm taking her down to the Crooked Spoon for a bowl of five-alarm chili."

"Sounds like a plan," replied Kreston, his footsteps echoing on the wooden floors.

Sadie sensed his overwhelming relief. Hearing his voice quickened her pulse—an effect growing stronger by the minute, despite her attempts to resist his pull on her.

"Oh, I love chili!" squealed Tess as they headed down the hallway. She hollered back at Sadie, "The check-in desk is closed, whatever your name is."

"Thanks, Tess, I'll remember that," Sadie hollered back.

"Her name is Sadie," Jessie patiently explained, their voices fading as they made their way down the stairs.

Sadie smiled, thankful Ten Second Tess was back to normal.

Janet shook Sadie's hand. "Quick thinking on your part, or the outcome might have been different. Thank you."

Sadie dismissed the compliment. "Anyone would have done the same."

"Well, you're the one who took action." Janet closed her medical bag and put on her coat. "I know you're new here, so please be careful in this cold. It's nothing to mess with. See you at the party tonight." Janet left the door open to Sadie's room and disappeared down the hall.

Exhausted, Sadie sank onto her bed and closed her eyes. She flopped backwards, her feet dangling toward the floor.

"Hey Seattle, how are you doing?" Concern etched the low rumble of Kreston's voice.

Sadie's eyes popped open to find him framed in her doorway like a knight in shining armor. She sat up and motioned toward an armchair and a side table in the corner. "Have a seat and help yourself to some tea."

"Thanks. Don't mind if I do." Kreston took a seat and filled a mug with tea.

"Thank you for finding Tess and for knowing what to do while the rest of us barked orders. Why were you walking outside in the snowstorm? How did you find her?"

"I took a walk because I wanted time to think," explained Sadie. "I passed Henrietta in front of Bob's Hardware store. She mentioned seeing Tess earlier at the playground, swinging on the swing-set, and going down the slide, so I thought it'd be fun to join her. But when I got there, I found her lying in the snow."

"I'm so glad you found her when you did." Kreston closed his eyes and let out a relieved sigh.

"Does anyone have responsibility for Ten Second Tess? Aloha said she had a brain injury a few years back. What's her story—how did she wind up here?"

Kreston sipped his tea. "Tess's story isn't a pleasant one. Her parents lived in Polar Creek but died in a plane crash when she was eighteen. She was the only survivor."

Sadie's eyes widened. "How horrible. How old is she now?"

"Twenty-three. But because Tess suffered a severe brain injury, she has the mental capacity of a child. Jessie had moved to town about that time and flew with me to visit Tess in the Fairbanks Hospital. When she was released, we brought her back to Polar Creek. Jessie took Tess under her wing, and she's lived with Jessie ever since. The brain injury left Tess with a short-term memory that lasts ten minutes at a time. Then it resets. Oddly, she always remembers me, Jessie, Tucker, and Lucky. Other than that, she doesn't remember anyone else."

Tears pooled in Sadie's eyes. "That's terrible. What an awful thing."

"Depends on how you look at it. Taking care of Tess saved Jessie in many ways. Gave her a reason to get up every day after what she'd been through. Tess remembers nothing about what happened, so she's a happy camper."

"We need a system for keeping track of Tess," suggested Sadie. "What do you think about using something like a GPS pendant or wristband to alert us if she wanders out of close range?"

His eyes lit up. "Great idea. Brilliant, in fact. I'll talk to Jessie about it." He pulled out his phone, then looked at her with sudden intensity. "You said we and us."

"I did?"

"Just now, when you suggested a way to keep track of Ten Second Tess."

Heat crept up her neck. "Force of habit and slip of the tongue."

"Right." He smirked, fidgeting with his phone. "Are we still on for the holiday party tonight?"

"You mean our date?"

He grinned. "I'll even pick you up from your room and escort you across the street, like a regular guy."

"Such a gentleman," she teased. "Escorting me a whole fifty feet."

"You never know what could happen in fifty feet." He shook his head. "Polar Creek gangs, wild-assed yeti like Bigfoot or Sasquatch...it's a jungle out there."

"More like a wild-assed tundra out there." She sat back, studying him. "You chose well. Leaving city life behind, I mean. Not sure I could do that." She looked down at her mug, running her finger around the rim.

When she looked up, he looked almost crestfallen.

*Oh no, I said the wrong thing.*

He set down his mug with a closed-mouthed smile. "Have a few things to do. Like prepare an Arctic char to cook for dinner, remember?"

Sadie chortled. "That's right. Got your vocal cords all tuned up?"

"Primed and ready. I hope it's a good song, like a rock ballad." He turned to face her. For a fleeting moment, Sadie hoped he would pick up where he left off earlier and kiss her. "Something like 'Bohemian Rhapsody,'" he murmured, close to her lips.

A giddy sensation tickled her, but her heart stuttered its own disappointment when he stepped back. "See you at dinner."

"Okay." She followed him to the door and stared after him as he walked down the hallway, studying his easy gait. He walked like he hadn't a care in the world.

She admired his straightforward, compassionate manner. Kreston knew what he wanted, despite muscling his way through physical and mental obstacles to attain it. Some life journeys were stumbling blocks, and it seemed she and Kreston had each done their share of stumbling around.

After he left, Sadie curled up in the chair, her mind spinning in confusion. When had these quirky but lovable people become more than just acquaintances? The Gossip Trio had appointed themselves as her personal romance advisors—when had that ceased to be an annoyance? The last couple of days had been a blur of delights—Lucky sharing stories about Kreston's early Alaska adventures, the unlikely victory in the Outhouse race with "the fastest toilet in the North," the sled dog race, and Tucker presenting her with the trophy fish while the town cheered.

What was not to like about all that?

But most of all...she'd won her bet with Kreston. And she couldn't wait to collect. Polar Creek may not be a detour after all. A random thought forced its way into her brain.

*Could it be she was already home?*

Suddenly, she couldn't bear the thought of leaving.

# Chapter 14

*K**reston*

"If you check your fish's temperature one more time," warned Jessie. "I'm going to let Ten Second Tess reorganize your clothes closet."

Kreston pulled back from the Crooked Spoon's kitchen grill, holding a long spatula. He aimed not to look as nervous as he felt. The Arctic char—Sadie's triumphant catch—deserved perfection.

"I just want to make sure it's cooked," he defended.

"Like how you control everything else in your life?" Jessie effortlessly managed three pasta pots while assembling holiday-themed salads. "Except it's not working out so well lately, is it? Not since a certain redheaded beauty blew into town."

Kreston had gotten used to Jessie's constant pounding of the Sadie drum, but he disliked being pushed into anything. "Don't know what you're talking about," he mumbled.

Lucky appeared in the kitchen doorway. "Why is your face red? Cooking fish too much for you?"

"Look how golden brown this is. Mm, it's a masterpiece." Kreston sampled a morsel.

"Can't wait to hear you sing. Only time I've heard you belt out a tune was during Polar Creek's Colony Days when you were sloshed, and no one understood a word. All right, buddy, the karaoke machine is ready to go. This'll be interesting." Lucky popped out again.

Kreston peeked out at the dining area to note the Crooked Spoon filling up like a TV game day when everyone gathered to watch the Seattle Seahawks. When Jessie and Aloha announced there would be fancy desserts at the holiday party, a cheer went up throughout the restaurant.

"This char won't be enough to feed everyone. Are you sure we have enough salmon?" Kreston twirled his spatula, his stomach curdling at the thought of singing. Though he'd performed in an a cappella group in college, he'd given up singing along with everything else when his life fell apart back East.

Sadie still hadn't told him what song she'd chosen. He feared croaking out the lyrics like a frog with laryngitis at an open mic night in Lilypad Marsh.

Jessie surveyed the crowd with hands on her hips. "Yep, we have plenty of fish. Hardware Bob and the Gossip Trio donated frozen salmon fillets just to make sure."

Kreston let out a sigh of relief. "Good. I didn't want a riot on my hands." He nodded toward the karaoke machine. "I suspect it's not only the fish drawing the entire town here. They just want to see me make a fool of myself."

Jessie laughed outright. "Poor baby. Cry me a river. Now get out there and help Sadie serve the masses. That was part of the bet, remember?" She returned to her job plating food.

"Right." Kreston found the large round tray and loaded five plates of food onto it.

Jessie brandished a long three-pronged fork. "Drop that food and there will be hell to pay."

Sadie appeared to collect more plates and grinned at Kreston. "Those people are chomping at the bit to hear their illustrious mayor serenade their dinner. Mm, this smells delicious. Good job on my fish." Sadie leaned across Kreston to snatch a plastic bottle of tartar sauce, and he caught a whiff of her expensive cologne.

Jessie sidled up to Sadie. "Did you know Kreston sang in a Harvard a cappella group?" she said out the side of her mouth.

"He what?" Sadie stopped, her jaw dropping.

"That was a long time ago." Kreston dismissed it with an eyeroll.

Lucky popped back into the kitchen. "Yeah, they wore matching blazers and everything."

"Just a few semesters, for charity fund-raisers." Kreston muttered, plating more fish. Plastering on a smile, he ducked out to avoid further disclosures from Jessie.

Lucky gave them both a hand, serving the fish. When everyone had their food, Sadie, Kreston, and Lucky sped between tables, supplying water and other beverages.

Sadie moved up to Kreston and handed him her moose antler hat. "You're on, buddy. Get up there and strut your stuff!" From the way her eyes glinted, she was obviously relishing this, making him even more edgy. He plopped the hat on his head with as much dignity as he could muster.

The Gossip Trio waved at him from their table, like three groupies. All three had hit on him at one time or another. He'd been careful about keeping his distance, yet maintaining good mayoral relations. The Trio turned out to be an informative group, helping him to keep his finger on the town's pulse.

"What are you going to sing, Mayor Collins?" Tall Martha clapped her hands, her enthusiasm in obvious overdrive.

When Sadie's song choice appeared on the karaoke screen, Kreston gulped as panic seized his throat, choking him. He narrowed his eyes and shot a fighting glance at her as she leaned against the wall with folded arms, a smirk playing across her face.

He shook his head with dread, as if he'd been asked to preside at his own funeral.

"That bad, huh?" Mini-Martha hollered, sending a titter of anticipation over the room.

Henrietta adjusted her glasses with a toothy grin. "Come on, Bing Crosby, croon your little heart out. Give us a 'White Christmas.' As if we don't have one." She motioned at the windows, and everyone laughed.

Kreston's chin dropped to his chest, and he squeezed his eyes closed. "All right, let's get this over with," he muttered under his breath, dragging a stool from the bar and perching himself on it.

He dipped a reluctant nod at Lucky, who stood ready to operate the karaoke machine.

The opening notes of Helen Reddy's "I Am Woman" filled the restaurant.

Every woman in the place burst out laughing, and while they clapped and cheered, Kreston's chest detonated with full-fledged terror. He darted another horrified look at Sadie, who was busy cracking up.

Kreston's first few halting notes were barely audible, but what happened next would become the stuff of Polar Creek legend. If he was going to do this, he might as well go all in with gusto and pour his heart and soul into it.

*What the heck.*

He summoned his inner holiday spirit, and his rich baritone transformed the song into something no one expected...least of all himself.

The shock on every face was priceless. The men sat stunned, while the women beamed as Kreston's voice echoed from the speakers, singing it like his own personal anthem.

The women clapped along and pumped their fists, shouting, "Oh yeah!"

Kreston noted Lucky's amused expression and Tucker shaking his head with a hand clasped over his mouth.

Aloha rushed up and joined in the singing. The Gossip Trio joined them, and soon a female chorus of "I Am Woman" drowned out Kreston's voice. He didn't mind—in fact, he was relieved and gladly stepped back to let the women take the spotlight. Even Ten Second Tess got into the spirit, though she couldn't quite keep up with the lyrics. Within moments, every woman in the restaurant was singing.

Kreston caught Sadie's eye as she clapped and sang along, her jubilant expression warming him. When the song ended, he motioned to the group who'd joined him. "Give these ladies a hand!"

The standing ovation was deafening. He thought he'd go up in flames as a man singing a woman's anthem. Instead, it had the opposite effect, especially when Henrietta yelled, "Mayor Collins, will you marry me?"

"Thanks, everyone. That was fun." Heat crawled up his neck as his wide smile captured the attention of every woman in the room. "Now, please finish eating. We have a holiday party to attend. With *real* musicians, I promise."

"Bravo! Bravo! Oh my, you were spectacular!" Tall Martha fanned herself. "Mayor Collins, please record an album so I can fall asleep to your singing and dream about you."

He figured she was teasing, but maybe not.

"Who knew?" Mini-Martha sighed, looking at Kreston like she was a groupie who came to every show.

Their remarks made him squirm, but he let them slide off. He knew their comments were all in good fun. Mostly.

Tucker imparted his existential philosophy. "Such is the duality of man, expressed through Helen Reddy."

As everyone paid their bill and straggled out of the restaurant, Sadie swaggered up to him. "Saved by your groupies," she teased. "They wound up doing the heavy lifting."

"Nuh-uh," he countered. "I sang the first few verses alone."

"And not too bad, actually." She gave him an assessing look. "You should sing more often."

"As you can see, I'm in touch with my feminine side," he joked.

"You're a good sport, Mayor Collins." Sadie's approval skittered his brain off somewhere.

"Let's clear these tables and help Jessie clean up." Kreston summoned Aloha and Ten Second Tess to help.

They set to work cleaning the tables and loading the oversized dishwasher. When things were situated, everyone scattered to get ready for tonight's holiday party. Kreston was glad he'd had the foresight to bring in his dress duds earlier. He was grateful to Lucky for volunteering to drive out and feed his sled dogs. One less thing Kreston had to worry about today, with his combined responsibilities.

Not only that, he was anxious about his date tonight. The word 'date' sounded so official.

Kreston casually excused himself and hurried out of the Crooked Spoon, with Sadie on his heels. "Be up in a few," he tossed at her as he rushed across the lobby toward his office to get changed.

"Okay, later," she replied, dashing up the stairs.

Kreston closed the door to his office and put on the tuxedo he'd dragged to Alaska from Manhattan years ago. "You never know when you'll need to dress up in the Alaskan wilderness," he'd joked to Lucky back then.

The shirt still fit, but the silky pants were tight, along with his suit jacket. He'd gained bulk from chopping wood and all the other physical activities that came with his Polar Creek lifestyle. The tux felt both foreign and familiar as he shrugged it on.

Peeking into a mirror in his one-horse bathroom with just a toilet and a sink, he smoothed back his hair and ran a shaver around his face. Studying his reflection, he noticed he'd aged since coming here. But in a good way. Not the old stress lines that used to crease his face when he worked in finance. He liked this new version of himself: the laugh lines around his eyes, the snow boots next to his desk, and the many hats he wore. He took pride in how he'd made a difference in this town.

A familiar tap-tap sounded on the door as he fiddled with his bow tie for the hundredth time.

Kreston swung open the door to find Jessie, who stepped back with a long, descending whistle. "Well, look at you, all gussied up like a man about town!" She grinned. "If I were twenty years younger, I'd make a play for you. Every woman in Polar Creek will eye you tonight like a fine cut of prime beef—just like they do at those Talkeetna bachelor auctions. Nice tux, by the way."

"Oh, this old thing?" he teased with a nervous laugh. "Thanks, nice of you to say."

She leaned against the doorframe with folded arms. "Haven't seen you this nervous since you told Ten Second Tess liquid soap didn't go in the coffeemaker."

"I'm not nervous," he insisted, fiddling unsuccessfully with his tie.

"I beg to differ." Jessie stepped in and moved his hands away to take over the tie operation, then she pointed at his feet. "You're wearing two different colored socks."

He glanced down and raised a pant leg. "Damn it."

"No one'll notice. Just giving you a hard time. Here." She straightened his tie with motherly precision. "The way Sadie helped Tess yesterday, then pitched in to help you serve fish tonight, even though she won the bet...not something to ignore."

He bobbed his head up and down impatiently. "I know, Jessie..."

"I don't think you do. All I'm saying is, Sadie is special. Don't let your fear and stubbornness stand in the way." She brushed away imaginary lint from his shoulders. "Remember that tonight when you dance with her. And try to relax and enjoy it. Tomorrow is Christmas Eve, and I hope you have a present for her."

"Yes, Mom. Any other pearls of wisdom for my first date?" He gave her his best teenage eyeroll, channeling every sixteen-year-old prepping for a prom.

"As a matter of fact, yes." Jessie planted her hands on her hips, switching into lecture mode. "A woman gives you a sign. You know, like when she wants to be kissed."

He groaned inwardly. *Dear God, we're actually having this conversation.*

"Enlighten me," he managed, his voice cracking traitorously.

"When Sadie does the lean-in with an I-want-to-make-out-with-you face, that's your cue. I know it's been a while—"

"Only a minute or two," he cut in, tapping his chin with mock solemnity. "Surprisingly, I still remember the basics of human mating rituals."

"Alrighty then, you're good to go. Have fun, Mayor Collins." She gave him a knowing wink and popped out of his office.

Kreston watched his good friend disappear down the hallway, appreciating Jessie's good intentions and how she always had his back. No, he didn't have a present for Sadie. He'd worry about that later. First, he had a date to focus on with this beautiful woman who'd captured his heart.

On his way upstairs to Sadie's room, Kreston glanced both ways before plucking a silk poinsettia from the lobby's holiday decorations. Real flowers were scarce around these parts at this time of year. This would have to do.

His flower tremored in his hand as he climbed the stairs, and his heart pounded as he approached Sadie's door. He'd weathered stock market crashes, faced bear encounters, dicey flight conditions, and angry townspeople, but this date terrified him more than he cared to admit—it threatened to do him in.

He stood for a moment outside Sadie's door to collect himself. He squared his shoulders, recalling what he'd learned back in business school: the scariest risks were the ones that paid off in the end. He hoped it was also true in relationships.

Kreston crossed his fingers, took a deep breath, and raised his hand to knock.

# Chapter 15

S*adie*
Sadie stood near the punch bowl, mesmerized by the multicolored lights simulating the Aurora dancing across the tall ceiling. Hardware Bob had outdone himself by setting up the display, creating an effect so realistic she could stare at it all night.

Bob appeared beside her, grinning proudly. "Took three days to rig everything just right. Ordered the parts from Anchorage and cost a fortune to ship them here. Worth it, though—we can enjoy the Aurora even when it's cloudy outside."

"It's beautiful," she admitted, her gaze shifting to Kreston, who stood talking to a group of people across the room.

When she opened her door, seeing him in a tuxedo had taken her breath away. He was a different man tonight—his usually windswept hair tamed as if he'd had it styled at a hair salon. She wondered if Polar Creek even had one. He appeared nervous, which had her wondering.

"You look nice tonight, Miss Sadie," said Hardware Bob, dipping into the punch.

"Thank you." Good thing she'd packed her sparkling black cocktail dress when planning to spend the holidays with her ex. Her peep-toe glittery stilettos set it off, and she'd had to cling to Kreston's arm, walking to the Polar Creek Community

Center. It wouldn't have been good form to take a header in the middle of Main Street. She'd even curled her hair, the first time using her curling iron since arriving here. It hung in loose spiral curls, framing her face and cascading down her back.

Kreston hadn't taken his eyes off her, but his nervousness mystified her. What was the deal with him?

The local band struck up "White Christmas" with Tucker on the piano, Hardware Bob's wife Janet on the fiddle, and Henrietta from the Gossip Trio, on guitar. The melody caressed Sadie like a warm blanket as couples drifted onto the floor.

"May I have this dance?" He stood straight and tall, like a towering spruce.

Sadie's heart stumbled at seeing Kreston before her, resplendent in his tux, his hand elegantly extended, blue eyes reflecting the waving lights. She hadn't danced since a fall fundraiser she'd attended with her ex at the Hyatt in Seattle. A thought occurred that Clayton was no match for the man standing before her.

Not even close. This guy had class in spades.

"Seeing as this is an official date, I'll dance with you," she replied, walking on a virtual cloud.

"Consider it a special addition to your cultural immersion in Polar Creek." His hand was warm as she took it.

She laughed easily. "I've experienced a lot of deep immersion here, thanks to you."

"I'm glad the blizzard landed you here." His smile deepened, creating dimples she'd noticed upon meeting him but had forced herself to ignore.

Her hand rested in his, and he closed his fingers around it. They were warm and slightly calloused, probably from working with his sled dogs or messing with his plane and the snowmachines. When he drew her into his arms, her body fit perfectly, as if they'd been dancing together for years.

Kreston danced with the nonchalant grace of someone who'd done this before, his movements smooth and elegant. Every gaze locked onto them as they danced. Sadie felt like an ice worm under a microscope, like the tiny black ones Kreston said lived inside of glaciers.

"Hardware Bob did an amazing job with these lights," she murmured, watching the electronic Aurora light show swirl around them.

"He insisted on getting it perfect. He does this for special occasions." He pressed her against him, and her pulse sped when his face came within inches of hers.

When their eyes met, the rest of the room faded away. His thumb traced circles on her back, sending tingles through her.

*God help me, I love the feel of him. I can't fall for him, I can't!*

The song ended, and the music became lively. They released each other to dance separately, much to Sadie's disappointment.

After "Rockin' Around the Christmas Tree" ended, Sadie fanned her face with her hand. "It's warm in here."

"How about some fresh air?" Kreston offered his elbow and led her to the back entrance.

The single back door opened onto a modest cedar deck behind the building, twinkling lights wrapped around the railing. Someone had cleared the snow. Probably Kreston.

"Look up!" he pointed.

The sky had cleared, and it finally stopped snowing. High above, the Aurora dazzled with bursts of green and red neon.

The light show exceeded Bob's indoor display, as if by design for tonight's party, creating multi-colored waves and swirling starbursts.

"Now that's timing," Kreston murmured, standing close enough she could feel his warmth in the frigid air. "Though I have to admit, Bob's version is more reliable."

"But less magical." Puffs of frost formed with every exhale.

"I wouldn't say that." He turned to face her, the sheer bulk of him causing her heart to bounce. "There's plenty of magic right here."

"You are stunning tonight. I'll keep you warm." He slipped his arm around her waist, and she leaned into him.

"You clean up well. Like *really* well." The frigid air caused her to shiver.

"You're cold." He removed his suit jacket and draped it around her shoulders.

"Thank you." She snuggled into his warm jacket, loving Kreston's scent. Her heart flip-flopped around in confusion, wanting to melt into him, knowing she shouldn't. She had to go Outside—back to Seattle.

"We should head back inside. But first, I want to do something." He drew her tight, turning her to face him.

"What?" She knew darn well what and closed her eyes in anticipation.

Before she could tick off the reasons this shouldn't be happening, his lips had found hers. The kiss was tentative and gentle at first, giving her every chance to pull away. But when she slid her hands up Kreston's chest, he deepened the kiss as the Aurora whirled above them.

Sadie's insides shifted as her permafrost heart thawed. Kreston kissed like he did everything else: with passion, control, and commitment. She didn't want this moment to end—it was the most romantic moment ever. Everything suddenly seemed clear.

*I could lose myself in Kreston forever.*

The thought sent panic whizzing through her like a tornado.

She jerked back, breathing hard. "Kreston—oh my God—I can't, this isn't..."

"Sadie? Should I not have done that?"

"Yes—I mean no. I can't do this." How could she explain she was falling for him? For this town? For this life that could never be hers?

Above them, the Aurora rippled, a witness to her unraveling: Seattle waited. Her career waited. Reality waited.

"I'm so sorry," she whispered and hurried down the steps, slipping and sliding, not caring if she ruined her heels in the snow.

"Sadie, wait! Come back!" The urgency in Kreston's voice tore her to pieces.

The fifty feet back to the hotel felt like fifty miles, each agonizing step causing her heart to crack a little more. On the way, she encountered Aloha, who'd run back to the hotel for another plate of cookies.

"Aloha, Sadie! You're going the wrong way!" Aloha hollered after her. "What's wrong?"

Kreston followed her to the middle of Main Street, still calling her name.

"No! I can't!" Tears rushed out. She turned to see his blurry form—and it destroyed her. She stumbled through the snow in her haste to get away.

Sadie swung open the door to the hotel and ran across the lobby, slipping on her saturated stilettoes. Tears came hot and fast as she ran upstairs, seeking sanctuary in her room.

Aloha's voice sounded in the hallway as she slammed and locked the door, leaning against it, sobbing.

"Sadie, Kreston wants you to come back to the party." Aloha knocked on her door. "Are you okay? Do you need help?"

"No, Aloha, I'm fine," she lied, sobs wracking her shoulders.

In her brief time here, these people had become like family: Jessie, with her motherly wisdom and stress-baking; Lucky with his terrible jokes and enormous heart. Tucker with his artistic philosophical observations. Ten Second Tess, with her eternal curiosity and confused thoughts; the Gossip Trio who enjoyed playing matchmaker. And Aloha, with her forgetfulness mixed with clarity.

Then there was Kreston. God, Kreston. The superhero who governed an entire town with grace and humor—who helped everyone without keeping score—and kissed like he was offering his heart along with his lips.

"What am I doing?" she whispered to the empty room. "What do I want?"

But she knew what she was doing... protecting herself...and protecting *him*. Staying would mean risking everything—her career, her heart, her civilized city life. Leaving Polar Creek would hurt, but at least it was a pain she could control.

Couldn't she?

Through her window, the northern lights continued their dance, mocking her for bailing on a second chance at love. Somewhere out there, Kreston stood under those same lights, trying to make sense of why she turned chicken and ran. How could she give him what he deserved—commitment, permanence, and a shared future in this town he loved so much and would never leave?

The sob heaved from her chest, surprising her with its force. She'd visualized all of it...starting over with a new life in this quirky, loving community. She'd envisioned spending mornings helping Jessie at the Crooked Spoon and evenings taking sled dog rides with Kreston. Holidays with these people would be like spending Christmas in Whoville.

After all, she'd become disillusioned with the way her public relations job had turned out. She was repulsed by those who'd slipped from the carefully crafted personas she'd built for the rich and famous—then demanded she fix their images after their infidelities and immoral behaviors. The whole thing had discouraged her, and it was the main reason she'd needed the holiday break. Her ex had been the one to suggest they fly north to Alaska. Now she didn't know whether to curse him or thank him for it.

The scariest thing wasn't outright rejection or losing love—she'd already experienced those. No, what terrified her was finding love again here—in the most impossible place she could have imagined. And the last place she ever thought to look.

Sadie buried her face in her pillow and let the tears flow out of her.

# Chapter 16

K *reston*

The next morning on Christmas Eve, Kreston numbly stared at the hotel's ledger. The numbers blurred into oblivion while his mind replayed last night's kiss and the way Sadie had melted into him. Then she'd mystified him by pulling away and left him standing in the cold with his heart in his hands.

He hadn't slept well, and he'd toyed with the idea of not even coming to work this morning. But he'd forced himself to drive in, knowing if Sadie peeked out the window, she'd see his truck and would know he was there. He kept glancing at the door, hoping she'd pop in to explain why the heck she'd bailed on him.

"You're obviously not with the program this morning," observed Jessie, appearing with coffee. "You look like a zombie with that neglected five o'clock shadow. Want to talk about it?"

"There's nothing to talk about." His voice was tinged with a sharp edge.

Jessie raised her brows. "Oh, is that right? Because Ten Second Tess ran into the party last night saying some lady was kissing Mayor Collins on the back deck. But ten minutes later, she couldn't answer questions from the Gossip Trio."

He cocked a brow, but before he could respond, his radio crackled: "Polar Creek, this is The Beave with the Christmas mail. Fifteen minutes out. Over."

"Copy that," replied Kreston, grabbing his coat and gloves. He'd left his boots on. "Meet you at the airstrip." He forced a smile for Jessie. "Time to put on my mail carrier hat."

"Have you talked to Sadie yet this morning?" Her stare drilled into him.

"It's early. She's still asleep." He squeezed past Jessie, then paused. "She ran off and left me last night, Jessie."

She heaved out a sigh. "I'll talk to her."

"She sure as heck doesn't want to talk to me," he mumbled.

"Did you tell her how you feel?"

A long moment of silence. "I kissed her. That communicated how I felt."

"But did you *tell* her how you feel?" Jessie pressed.

"Didn't get around to that," he mumbled, walking away from her. "Gotta go, see you later."

The drive out of town gave him too much time to think. He turned last night over and over in his mind, always coming to the same conclusion: Sadie bolted because she didn't want to get involved. He wasn't stupid; he knew why. But it still didn't lessen the sting of rejection.

Hadn't he done a similar thing when his life had blown up in a shit storm? Run away from his failed commitments after the woman he'd intended to marry broke it off? Sadie had her career, and he had his. Her life was in the city, his was not. End of story.

Kreston climbed out of his pickup as the sun peeked over in a blaze of yellow, lighting up the white mountains. He put on his pilot shades, staring into the brightening blue. It was a beautiful day for flying. Not a cloud in the sky, and winds were relatively calm. He heard Lucky's DeHavilland Beaver before seeing the speck flying over the mountains coming toward him.

Lucky's skis touched down in a spray of snow, and silence descended when the propellor stopped. He emerged from the pilot seat.

"Special delivery. One plane load of Christmas cheer!" he said in his Irish lilt, opening the cargo hold.

*Glad someone is cheerful today. It certainly isn't me,* Kreston thought glumly.

"How was it near the Alaska Range?" he asked, as lively as he could muster.

"Beautiful. The Beave floated in the air like a balloon." Lucky stacked several boxes and handed them to Kreston. "Better get these delivered today, Kress. It's Christmas Eve."

"Yep, planning on it." Kreston stuffed the mail pouch into the truck's back seat.

They worked in companionable silence for a while, loading packages into Kreston's truck. Finally, Lucky cornered him, as Kreston knew he would.

"Want to tell me why you walked back into the party alone last night without your jacket? Or the girl?"

"Women." Kreston shook his head, hefting another box with more force than necessary. "They act interested, then, when you get down to brass tacks—bam! Rejection guts you like a salmon."

"Ah." Lucky nodded sagely. "The old 'kiss and run.' Classic holiday romance maneuver."

"I guess so." Kreston blew out air, creating frosty vapor. "I never stood a chance with her from the get-go. This isn't a Hallmark Christmas movie where the city girl stays with the country boy."

Lucky wrinkled his face. "You watch that stuff?"

"Jessie subscribed to that Galaxy-Link satellite streaming network and plays those movies constantly on the hotel kitchen TV," explained Kreston defensively. "Can't help seeing them whenever I stop in."

"Uh-huh, I'll believe it when you buy a bridge to nowhere," joked Lucky. "Back to Sadie. She asked me to fly her to Talkeetna, where she'll pick up the train to Anchorage."

"When are you taking her?"

"First, I have to take a run to McGrath to bring back the Simenson family," explained Lucky. "Remember how they fly home each Christmas to spend the holiday with their kids? When I get back, I'll load up Sadie and her gear and fly her to Talkeetna."

The package in Kreston's hands suddenly felt like an anvil. "Wish she would have asked me to take her, but I can understand why she didn't." It still smarted. Maybe she didn't trust his flying. He should have taken her up in his plane, but with the ongoing storm, it hadn't been an option.

"She's running," Lucky stated matter-of-factly. "Question is, are you going to let her?"

"I have no say in her decisions or what she does. What am I supposed to do? She has a life in Seattle. I have responsibilities here, and that's all there is to it."

Lucky grimaced. "Bullheaded, much? I haven't seen you in this good of a mood since we got your plane started after being stranded on Ruth Glacier with those Denali climbers. You ought to give this a bit of thought."

"It's not that simple."

"Never is." Lucky threw his arms up. "That's why they call it taking a chance. You know what I think? You aren't afraid she'll leave...you're afraid she'll stay." He started his pre-flight check.

"You're not making sense," spluttered Kreston, even though his buddy had hit the proverbial nail on the head. The truth slammed into his chest like a rocket.

"Love rarely does. Just ask Ten Second Tess." Lucky grinned. "She told me this morning that hearts are like soup—warm and messy, sometimes spilling on your shirt. She may have a split-second memory, but she dispenses pearls of wisdom now and again."

Despite everything, Kreston smiled. "She said that?"

"Well, not in those exact words. But I'm a good interpreter." Lucky gave him a direct look. "If I were you, I'd skedaddle into town to catch Sadie before I fly her out of here. Okay?"

Kreston saw his point. "All right. You convinced me."

"Now help me refuel so I can get this bird in the air." Lucky pointed a thumb toward the hangar.

After Lucky took off, Kreston drove to his place to check on his sled dogs. In the meantime, he had to sort the packages—some for delivery and the rest for the post office—but talking to Sadie before she left was a matter of urgency.

His phone buzzed with a text from Jessie.

*Remember when you found me crying in the Anchorage diner? You told me I wasn't running away, that I was running toward a better life. Maybe it's time you take your own advice.*

Kreston read the message three times, his dogs watching with wagging tails as if they knew what it said.

He addressed his wagging dogs, lined up on top of their doghouses. "Okay, you guys. You win. I'll talk to Sadie first, before delivering the mail."

# Chapter 17

S*adie*

Sadie's fingers traced the lapel of Kreston's suit jacket, still draped over her armchair where she'd left it last night after fleeing the party. The fabric held his scent—pine and wood smoke, uniquely him. A tear splashed onto the dark material.

"Knock it off," she muttered to herself, shoving another sweater into her suitcase. "Stop crying over a man you barely know. Stop crying over a life you can't have," she chastised herself.

But that was the problem, wasn't it?

*I do know him.*

She knew his careful competence and hidden vulnerability. Knew how he checked on Ten Second Tess five times a day without making her feel monitored. Loved how his eyes crinkled when he laughed at Lucky's lame jokes.

And she knew she'd fallen in love with him.

"Sadie, are you all right in there?" Aloha lightly knocked on her door. "Don't be sad. Kreston likes you. Want some coffee? Or tea?"

Even Aloha knew.

*Am I that transparent?*

"Thanks, Aloha, I'm fine," she lied through the closed door. "I'm just—I'm just getting ready for breakfast." She'd miss Aloha's bursts of enthusiasm.

Lucky wouldn't be back for hours. She should return Kreston's jacket and try to explain why she ran from him last night. But the thought of facing him made her chest tight. What could she say?

*Sorry I fled after the best kiss of my life, but I'm terrified of getting hurt again? Sorry I'm falling for you, but I have a career in Seattle, and you're married to this town?*

Her phone buzzed—another message from her assistant about upcoming PR campaigns. She glanced down at the plethora of texts erupting from her phone. Polar Creek's spotty cell service must be working today. During the snowstorm, the service was down. She'd actually enjoyed not having to reach for her phone every two seconds while she'd been here.

"I'll deal with this when I get back to Seattle," she muttered, shoving the phone into her purse. She retrieved it again, curious whether Kreston might have texted.

She glanced through the texts. None from the mayor of Polar Creek. Then she realized he probably didn't have her number.

Grabbing the jacket, she headed downstairs. Kreston's office was empty, his usual precision evident in the neat stacks of papers. A photo on his desk caught her eye: the whole town gathered in front of the hotel, everyone beaming. A family portrait.

The post office was similarly deserted, with only a cheerful note on the door: "Making postal deliveries!" in his precise handwriting. She hung his jacket on the doorknob. This ultimate gesture cracked her heart wide open.

The Crooked Spoon beckoned with warmth and the smell of cinnamon rolls.

Jessie looked up from wiping tables. "Sit," she commanded. "Coffee first, then we'll talk about why you're wearing your resting runaway face."

They settled into a corner booth and Jesse poured them each a mug of coffee. Sadie stared into the steaming cup, wishing it held the answers to her confused state of mind. She lifted her gaze to Jessie's.

"Why does he do it?" she finally asked. "Be everything to everyone? It's like Polar Creek can't function without him."

"It's more like he can't imagine life without Polar Creek," explained Jessie. "He needs to feel needed. After Wall Street, after Sarah left him, he wanted to go somewhere he could rebuild himself and succeed—where he had better control of his destiny."

"Sarah?"

"His fiancée in Manhattan. When everything crashed, she crashed right along with his bank account. He came here looking for redemption and found family and stability."

"So, he's entrenched here on this hamster wheel of responsibility?" It was a bitter reality for Sadie, but then what did she expect?

"He chose this life." Jessie studied her. "Question is, what are you choosing?"

"I have a life in Seattle. A career. Responsibilities."

"Sounds familiar." Jessie's smile was gentle. "You know what I see? Two people afraid of taking chances and failing without even trying. That's the saddest thing. You'll never know what might have been."

"Life is a never-ending universe of choices, though, isn't it? Every second, every minute, must be decided. We rarely have the luxury to obsess over what might have been with every single decision." She shook her head dismally. "I already lost one man I loved. Don't want a repeat performance."

Jessie let out a long sigh. "If it's any consolation, Kreston also lost the person he intended to marry. It appears the two of you are on a level playing field, locked in an even score. Kreston isn't the kind who'd be unfaithful. It's just not in his wheelhouse." Jessie sipped her coffee. "Give this some thought, okay? That's all I'm saying."

Sadie blew out a long stream of air, watching the morning regulars trickle in.

Aloha waltzed to their table and got right to the point. "Mayor Kreston really, really, really likes you, Miss Sadie. Please don't go." She enveloped Sadie in a hug that smelled like coconut and coffee.

Aloha stepped back. "Everyone likes you and will be sad if you leave."

"Thanks, Aloha." Sadie fought tears as her careful defenses cracked.

Polar Creek had everything she now craved—community, friendships, belonging. And she was running from it because...why? Because long-distance relationships were hard? Because staying meant risking her heart completely? Or because staying meant admitting her perfect life in Seattle wasn't what she wanted after all?

That thought had niggled her even before she left home.

As Sadie watched the town through the frosted window, waking up to get on with the business of Christmas Eve, she noted how easily everyone moved in each other's orbits, like a Venn diagram. The weight of her decision to leave grew heavier.

This was Kreston's world. His responsibility. His redemption. What right did she have to complicate it?

"Lucky radioed. He has a Polar Creek couple he has to pick up in McGrath," explained Jessie. "He'll be back in a few hours. Still want the flight to Talkeetna?"

Sadie slowly nodded, not trusting her voice. Caring about people sometimes meant that the best thing you could do was to step back and let them go.

Even if every step felt like walking on broken glass.

# Chapter 18

K*reston*

Kreston fired up the engine in his pickup and started toward town when his radio crackled. "Mayor Collins? This is Janet. Do you copy?"

Cell phones were a hit and miss in Alaska's remote towns and villages, though companies forever promised to provide Polar Creek with better cell service. Until then, he advised residents to keep the old-fashioned way of communicating with CB radios.

Kreston retrieved the mic from his radio unit. "This is Mayor Collins. Janet, what's up?"

"Bob has had a heart attack. He's conscious, but he needs medical help beyond what I can provide. Jessie said you were out this way. Any chance you can stop by?"

"Yes, I'll be right there." He returned the mic and frowned. Just last week, he'd gently commented to Hardware Bob about losing weight when he huffed and puffed in and out of the Crooked Spoon. Didn't help he had bacon and fried eggs every morning for breakfast.

Kreston gunned it, slipping and sliding down the snowy road. He hadn't had time to plow it after the storm dumped two more feet. With the multitude of holiday activities, routine tasks often fell by the wayside. He pulled into the wide driveway leading to Hardware Bob's fancy digs. Owning a hardware store had its benefits.

Janet opened the door and invited Kreston inside. She led him to the couch where Bob lay, his face contorted and his breathing shallow and pained.

"Thanks for coming so soon, Mayor Collins. Bob needs a medivac. Can Lucky fly us to Anchorage?" Janet searched his face.

"He's gone to McGrath, but I can fly you," he volunteered, his mind ticking through what he'd have to do. "Get his winter gear on, and we'll load him into my truck."

"Thank you so much, Mayor." Janet grabbed her and Bob's coat and boots, then Kreston assisted her in getting Bob into his down parka.

They hooked Bob's arms over their shoulders and half-dragged, half-carried him to the pickup, where they loaded him into the back seat. Janet climbed in with Bob's head in her lap. Kreston sped back to the airstrip and pulled up next to the hangar. He skidded the truck to a halt and hopped out.

"Let's get Bob into the back seat of my plane," he instructed Janet.

They eased him out and got him on board. Janet sat in the back, cradling Bob's head in her lap, while Kreston moved his pickup out of the way, then topped off the plane's tank with av-gas.

The pre-flight checklist grounded him in his routine, even as his thoughts raced. Fuel level good. Oil pressure good. Systems checked green across the board. Lucky had promised clear skies, but Kreston had learned the hard way to always check Alaska's wait-a-minute weather. He studied the forecast from Polar Creek to Anchorage—he wouldn't let treacherous conditions blindside him. No flurries. No crosswinds. Finally, something going his way.

Kreston cranked the engine, spun the propellor, and turned on the heat. He handed Janet a set of headphones with a hot mic. Once she put them on, he asked her, "How's Bob doing?"

"Holding his own, but we need to hurry," urged Janet, her voice tremoring.

"Don't worry, I'll have you there in a jiff. Which hospital, Regional or Providence?" he spoke into his mic, turning to position his aircraft. He powered up the engine and taxied down the snowy airstrip.

"Whichever is closest to where we land," she replied in a shaky, worried voice.

"Sorry about these bumps." He didn't want to cause Bob any more discomfort than was necessary, but there was no way to avoid some jostling as the plane picked up speed.

Kreston lifted one wheeled ski, then the other, and they were airborne. He guided his plane smoothly into the crystal-clear morning and the big blue. Below them, Polar Creek grew smaller, and the highlands took over.

As his DeHavilland Beaver floated over the snow-laden mountains, Kreston nudged the throttle forward and banked the plane to the left toward Anchorage. The engine hummed steadily as the Alaska Range spread before him like nature's Christmas card.

He settled into his pilot rhythm—altitude, heading, airspeed....until Sadie interrupted his thoughts. That happened more often than not these past few days. He glanced back at

Janet. She was a trooper, holding Bob's head steady as Kreston increased his airspeed.

"Doing okay back there?" he asked.

"He's still breathing, and his heart is still beating," reported Janet. "I'm praying he makes it."

"Don't worry, he will." Kreston wished he knew for sure, but he wasn't a doctor. "It's clear sailing all the way to Anchorage."

At cruise altitude, the December air was smooth as silk. Kreston kept one eye on his instruments, the other on the spectacular view. The rugged Talkeetna Mountains gleamed in front of him, the morning sun glittering glaciers into rivers of silver.

Kreston tuned into Anchorage's radio frequency. "Merrill Field, this is DeHavilland N565TA, do you copy?"

"N565TA, this is Merrill, go ahead."

"Kreston Collins here, on a medevac from Polar Creek," he reported, his voice steady despite his urgency. "Cardiac event with a sixty-eight-year-old male. ETA is one hour and ten minutes. Requesting an ambulance to meet us at Merrill Field."

"Copy that. We'll be expecting you. Merrill clear," said the woman on the other end.

"N565TA, clear." He twisted to see Janet and gave her a thumbs up. Dammit, he thought. He wouldn't see Sadie before she left, but it couldn't be helped.

He switched the radio to his local frequency. "DeHavilland N420TA, this is N565TA. Lucky, you copy?"

Lucky's voice came back. "N565TA, what's up?"

"Flying Hardware Bob and wife Janet to Anchorage. Heart attack. Can you..." He hesitated, his eyes on the empty passenger seat, picturing Sadie there. "Will you please tell Sadie I had an emergency and—tell her goodbye for me?"

He envisioned Jessie hovering around the Crooked Spoon kitchen radio, listening to his transmission. She'd no doubt tell Sadie before Lucky got the chance.

"I'll tell her," Lucky's voice crackled through. "However, some things shouldn't be conveyed through intermediaries. Not even devastatingly handsome Irish ones."

Kreston let it hang there. "Thanks, Luck."

"Sure, buddy. DeHavilland N420TA clear."

Kreston flew the rest of the way in anxious silence, his navigation screen displaying the aeronautical route over the magnificent Matanuska-Susitna Valley, while Janet murmured soft encouragement to her husband. The empty co-pilot's seat bothered him—Sadie would have known what to say to keep everyone calm. She'd handled Ten Second Tess's crisis smoothly and efficiently, the way she undoubtedly dealt with her clients in the lower forty-eight.

"Merrill Field, this is the Polar Creek medevac. We're ten miles northwest."

"Polar Creek medevac, descend straight onto the main runway. We've cleared all traffic for your emergency."

Kreston ticked through his descent checklist. Below them, the Mat-Su Valley spread out in pristine white, dotted with the gray ice of lakes and ponds. Not how he'd planned to spend Christmas Eve—he'd thought of flying Sadie around Mount Denali—if she'd stayed.

Cook Inlet slid into view, its waters dark and dotted with chunks of ice big enough to land on. Anchorage sprawled along the coastline, the city's grid pattern clear in the early afternoon light.

"Janet, make sure Bob's secure. Landing in five minutes."

Kreston's hands moved through the familiar patterns—power back, wing flaps down, trim adjusted. The city grew larger as he lined up his DeHavilland to land. Ambulance lights flashed near the small terminal and the Merrill Field traffic control tower, letting him know they were ready for Bob.

The landing was one of his smoothest, as if his aircraft sensed what was at stake. His wheels took over, and he taxied the plane toward the ambulance. Kreston caught his reflection in the windscreen—the focused pilot who could handle any emergency stared back at him.

*So, I can handle this, but why can't I tell Sadie how I feel about her?*

EMTs swarmed his airplane as soon as he rolled it to a stop next to the Merrill control tower and cut the engine. He unbuckled and hopped out to open the rear door and give them a hand. The paramedics expertly helped Bob and Janet out, then strapped Bob to a gurney and loaded him into the ambulance.

In the controlled chaos of the transfer, Kreston's cell phone sounded, and he tapped it. "Hey buddy, I'm preparing to fly to Talkeetna. Are you on your way back?"

"Not yet. Still in Anchorage. Just dropped off Bob and Janet."

"How is he?"

"He stayed alive until we got here, so hopefully he'll be okay," replied Kreston.

"Wish I could delay my flight till you get here, but as you know, I'm not certified to fly IFR for night flying," said Lucky.

"Right." Kreston's heart dropped. "Bad timing. Tell Sadie—uh, tell her to have a pleasant trip home," he stammered.

"Copy that," replied Lucky. "Have a good flight back."

"You, too." Kreston ended the call, his heart clenching as he watched the ambulance pull away, red flashes reflecting off the snow. After a quick hug, Janet had gone along, too, leaving him alone with his thoughts and a plane that suddenly felt empty.

He wished he were running his dogs right now, or removing Ten Second Tess's mistletoe from the ice maker, or telling Sadie she was...what was she exactly? Someone he liked a lot? That sounded cheesy and sophomoric. Maybe was falling in love with? Couldn't be love if he'd only known her a little over a week—could it? He wasn't a fan of that insta-love stuff, but hey, miracles could happen. Maybe he should go with the feeling.

Merrill Field Tower cleared his aircraft for take-off. As he ticked through his pre-flight checks, Kreston's heart sank with the realization he wouldn't make it back to Polar Creek in time to see Sadie. Some things just weren't in the cards.

Anchorage gleamed below him as he became airborne. The sun had dipped low enough to shed a rosy alpenglow on Denali, resembling the world's largest pink-bubble-gum snow cone.

Today wasn't what he had in mind for Christmas Eve. Not by a longshot. But tonight could be.

He made a decision. Now he had to act on it.

# Chapter 19

S*adie*

"Ready to go, Miss Sadie?" Lucky appeared in Crooked Spoon's doorway, unusually subdued. "Weather's perfect. Christmas miracle after the storm."

Sadie's heart leaped. "Is Kreston back from Anchorage? Jessie heard he had to medevac Bob with a heart attack."

"Not yet. He's still an hour away." Lucky's Irish lilt carried genuine concern. "I'm sorry I have to fly you before Kreston gets here, but it can't be helped. I'm not certified for night flying." He gave her a tentative look. "Want to wait until tomorrow?"

"Oh, no, tomorrow is Christmas, and I don't want to infringe on your holiday. Let's go now." Sadie wanted more than anything to wait until tomorrow, but even then, she'd only be prolonging the inevitable. It would be agonizing, saying goodbye to Kreston.

Lucky and Jessie helped Sadie load her two large bags and carry-on into the truck bed of Kreston's pickup. Lucky had borrowed it from the airstrip lot, saying he figured it would be more comfortable. After nearly coming undone when Aloha pleaded with Sadie to stay and hugged her tighter than she'd been hugged since she couldn't remember when, she'd ducked into the back seat to avoid saying goodbye to anyone else.

Sadie's thoughts were so jumbled, the drive to the airstrip was a blur. After boarding and buckling herself inside the Beave, she put on her sunglasses and nervously fidgeted with her phone.

As Lucky ran through his pre-flight checks and refueled his plane, Sadie had the sudden urge to shout, "Yes, I want to wait until tomorrow!"

Something held her back. She had a life to go back to, and she'd convinced herself she'd better get on with it. In the meantime, her phone had blown up with more texts and emails from panicked clients—when weren't they panicking over an infraction or a screw-up?

She powered off her phone, her heart weighing heavier than when she'd first arrived, but she didn't want Lucky to see her angsty confusion.

Her departure flight from Polar Creek was worlds apart from her terrifying arrival. Today was a gorgeous, sunny day, displaying Alaska in all its beyond-description majesty. As they climbed above Polar Creek, Sadie pressed her face to the passenger window, completely understanding what had drawn Kreston to this wild place.

"It's different when you see this from a big-picture angle, isn't it?" Lucky's voice came through her headset. "That first flight, you were too busy writing your obituary to appreciate the view."

She couldn't help laughing. "If you recall, it was a raging blizzard. I was amazed you found Polar Creek. Let alone where to land."

"Check out The Great One at three o'clock." Lucky banked the plane slightly so she could take it in.

Denali rose alongside them like a dream made solid, its massive face catching the winter sun. Twenty thousand feet of rock and ice, dwarfing everything around it and overwhelming the landscape.

"Kreston had proposed building a hotel below us because of this view," Lucky intoned, pointing down. "But when he became mayor and took on other responsibilities, he figured it was too much."

"I envy you both with your friendship. Wish I had a friend like that." She ached, recalling seeing Denali for the first time with Kreston as they stood on Grayling Lake.

Lucky shot her a sidelong look. "You could...if you would give it a chance."

She didn't respond. Even though he didn't say Kreston's name, his words were daggers to her soul and her aching heart. She turned toward the side window to fix her gaze on Denali. Her thoughts returned to Kreston and the first time she saw this spectacular mountain. She mostly remembered the details, like when he'd lowered his sunglasses to look at her. His deep pools matched the sky, and she'd lost herself in them.

The mountain seemed to follow their flight the rest of the way to Talkeetna, a shadow looking over their shoulders, watching over their journey like a guardian. Below them, valleys carved by ancient glaciers wound between peaks like white rivers. The landscape was both brutal and beautiful.

"Kreston talked about flying his mail routes, discovering Polar Creek, and how he started his life over again," she offered as a way of loosening the tightness she felt in her chest.

"The first time Kreston and I flew this route," volunteered Lucky, "he was so quiet I thought something was wrong. Turns out he was seeing things clearly for the first time in years. Alaska has a way of baring your soul, showing you what matters."

Talkeetna appeared below them, nestled between rolling hills of snow-heavy spruce and birch. The Susitna River, a shimmering ribbon of silver, cut through the breathtaking landscape. Denali caught the sunlight as shadows gathered in the valley in the late afternoon.

Lucky set the plane down gently on the cleared runway, his wheels taking over the smooth landing.

"What an amazing flight! Thank you, Lucky," gushed Sadie, not wanting it to end. "These mountains are so much bigger than our Cascades in Washington."

"Only the best for our Seattle visitors." Lucky taxied the plane to a stop. "Mountains teach us about permanence. And spiritual growth." He cut the engine.

Sadie watched the propellor slow to a stop and glanced at him. "Thank you so much for flying me here." She opened her wallet, removing several hundred-dollar bills. "Here's for your fuel. I don't expect you to fly me here for free."

Lucky held up his hand. "Nope. Won't take your money. Consider it a Christmas present."

"But—" she protested, stopping when he opened the door and hopped out. She shoved the money into her purse.

Lucky swung open her door and offered his hand to help her. She took it and climbed out, then gave him a hug. "I'll miss you, Irish Guy, and your amusing jokes."

"The whole town will miss you. You brought us a fair amount of class and sass, along with a bit of *craic* once you settled in." He sounded wistful.

"Thanks for bringing me to Polar Creek. The holiday festival was a lot of fun." She did her best to hide the ache in her chest.

Sadie tapped her phone to call the Denali Roadhouse and request a lift. She turned to Lucky. "Okay, I'm all set. They're sending a shuttle to pick me up." She'd been dreading the finality of all this, like saying goodbye to a dear friend...which she supposed he was.

Lucky rested a hand on her shoulder. "I know I speak for all of Polar Creek when I say we enjoyed having you stay with us. Please come back for a visit. You'll always be welcome."

"I will. Thank you." She forced back tears, reminding herself that this was her decision. The problem was, she didn't know whether it was the right one.

*How does anyone ever know?*

While Sadie waited near the tiny terminal building, she watched Lucky climb in and take off for his return to Polar Creek. She gazed at the red and white plane until it became a tiny speck and disappeared altogether.

Well, that was the end of it.

The shuttle driver deposited her at the magnificent front door of the spacious main lodge of the Denali Roadhouse. It was right out of a Christmas card, its rustic exterior decked out with holiday decorations.

Sadie swung open the tall wooden door with the thick brass handle, and the driver brought in her bags. She tipped him, then moved to the check-in desk.

"Hello, I'm Sadie Foster." She smiled at the woman with long blonde curls.

"Ah yes, Sadie from Polar Creek?"

"Oh, I'm not from Polar Creek," Sadie rushed to explain. "I'm from Seattle. I mean, I was in Polar Creek, but I'm not from there. I was supposed to stay here a week ago." She didn't have the energy to explain. "It's a long story."

"Welcome, I'm Rochelle. And before you ask—yes, *that* Rochelle. Kreston's ex." She extended her hand. "I assume you met Kreston Collins."

# Chapter 20



Sadie's brows shot up in surprise. "Oh, small world. Yes, I recall someone named Kreston." She did her best to sound nonchalant.

"Let's get you checked in, then I'll direct you to your room upstairs. I upgraded you to the full-frontal view of Denali on the third floor since few people are here right now." She peered down at her computer. "You had a reservation for two. The other person isn't...?"

Sadie shook her head. "The other person cheated on me, so I told him not to bother showing up." It was easier to say now that time had passed.

"How awful. Sorry that happened." Rochelle hesitated. "How about a glass of wine in front of the fire once you're settled in?" She motioned at the enormous fireplace along one wall, with overstuffed furniture arranged in front of it.

"Actually, I would love it. Be down in fifteen." Sadie was curious to know more about Rochelle and Kreston. She wasn't about to pass up this unlikely opportunity.

"See you then." Rochelle smiled and picked up a ringing phone.

Sadie rode the elevator upstairs to the third floor, where she found the driver waiting with her bags. She couldn't believe it when she entered the spacious room and was immediately drawn to the front window where Denali filled the view. She tipped him again for her bags, and he thanked her and closed the door behind him.

"What were the chances of bumping into an old girlfriend of Kreston's?" she wondered out loud. Of course, she'd have wine with her. She thought of what Kreston always said: does a moose drop nuggets?

She changed into jeans and a red cashmere sweater. When she peered at her reflection in the bathroom mirror, she looked gloomy. She applied eyeliner, mascara, and pink lipstick to perk herself up before heading for the elevator and down to the lobby.

Rochelle sat in an overstuffed chair, talking with guests. She pointed to a glass of white wine on the table as she finished her conversation.

Sadie took the chair next to her and helped herself to the wine. A saucer of cheese and crackers sat next to it, and she nibbled on a piece of Havarti.

When the other guests left, Rochelle turned to her. "So, let me guess. You and Kreston hit it off, didn't you?"

Sadie spluttered her sip of wine, choking on it. "Uh, why do you say that?"

"It's written all over you." She grinned. "No one as beautiful as you could go to Polar Creek and emerge without hooking up with its charming mayor, hot postal clerk, and beloved hotel manager."

"Oh, but we didn't hook up," Sadie rushed to say. "And you forgot he's also a—"

"Bush pilot," Rochelle finished for her. "Kreston is driven to be all things to all people, or he isn't happy."

Sadie appreciated hearing this. "All right, fill me in. I want to know more about him."

Rochelle repeated what Kreston had told her in the ice fishing shack: all about the exiled Wall Streeter who'd turned his redemption into a mission to save others.

"We went out several years ago, only for about four months, until I took the job here,"

Rochelle explained. "You should have seen Kreston when he first arrived in Polar Creek. Designer shoes completely ruined by snow, putting on a tough guy act, like losing what he had hadn't destroyed him. But he resonated with the wilderness vibe."

Through the window, Denali was still visible, a sentinel painted in alpenglow. Even here, the mountain seemed to watch over her—a constant reminder of Kreston.

Rochelle sipped her wine. "The thing about Kreston is, he didn't just accept help from Polar Creek. His quest became something bigger. Every person he's helped since—Tucker, Jessie, Aloha, Ten Second Tess—they're his way of making up for failure."

"By trying to fix everyone's problems," finished Sadie. "Jessie said the same thing."

"He created a place where broken things can heal. Including himself." Rochelle's expression grew thoughtful. "He used to say he felt closest to himself when flying near Denali. How problems that seemed huge on the ground seemed insignificant from up there."

She hesitated, giving Sadie a long look. "Are you—do you care for Kreston?"

The question caught Sadie off guard, and she wasn't sure how to answer. "Well, I...I, yes, but it's complicated."

"Always is. I feel you, though. Back when we dated, he was solid in his stance about staying in Polar Creek. I didn't want to stay." Rochelle shrugged. "We weren't serious, so it wasn't hard for me to leave."

"Yeah. Only, I couldn't stay because I have a life in Seattle. A high-paying job I'm good at. A beautiful condo..." she trailed off, sounding lame.

"Who's to say whether you're making a right or wrong decision? Just make sure it's what your heart wants," cautioned Rochelle. "So you'll have no regrets later on."

"Thanks for the advice." Sadie finished her wine. "I should get to bed. I'm taking the early train to Anchorage in the morning. Thought I'd ride the train since I won't be coming back to Alaska."

Rochelle gave her a doubtful look. "You sure about that? You know what they say—once you visit Alaska, you'll always return. I wouldn't be so sure."

"I'm not sure about anything anymore. I'm not even sure I want to go back to my job." Sadie didn't know why she leaked that little tidbit. Must be the wine, loosening her tongue. "It was so nice meeting you, Rochelle. Thanks for the wine. And the wisdom."

"Safe travels home," replied Rochelle, rising and taking both glasses. "If you want a bite to eat, Eagle's Perch restaurant is open until ten. Merry Christmas."

"Thanks. Merry Christmas to you, too." It was odd to say that here where she was alone, after being besieged every minute of the day by a Polar Creek resident. Christmas would only be another day since she'd be traveling. Then, when she arrived home to her condo, she could brood about being alone.

She suddenly thought of Ten Second Tess, hoping Kreston would remember to equip her with some sort of GPS tracker. When Sadie reached her room, she fished her laptop from its case and Googled the email address of the Polar Creek Mayor's office. She found it on a State of Alaska website and composed a message. The cursor blinked accusingly as she struggled to find the words:

*Dear Kreston, I now understand why you chose to live in Polar Creek. I truly saw Alaska today for the first time. The majesty and raw beauty that humbles yet exhilarates you. I get why you stayed. What I don't understand is why I left...*

She pounded the 'delete' key, teardrops splashing her keyboard. Kreston was probably back in Polar Creek by now.

Through the window, Denali's shadow stretched over the landscape like a sundial, marking time she couldn't get back. Random thoughts ticked through her brain as she watched the last light fade from the mountains. Each second ticked her further away from Polar Creek. She thought about her rigid work schedule, managing crises for those willing to pay dearly for her services. She thought of Polar Creek, its chaos and heart, and the people who saw worth in broken things.

And Kreston's kiss.

Jessie's words from this morning ticked back and forth in Sadie's mind like a metronome: "You'll never know what might have been."

Shaking off her loneliness, she abruptly stood, not wanting to be alone. She'd go downstairs and get a bite to eat.

At least in the restaurant, she'd be surrounded by the clatter of dishes and the murmur of other people's conversations...but none like the ones in Polar Creek.

# Chapter 21

K*reston*

Kreston had never chased after anyone in his life. Not in his Manhattan days, when women were drawn to his success like mosquitoes to tourists. And not in Polar Creek, where his chick-magnet charm made him every woman's favorite bachelor. He'd always been pursued, never the pursuer.

Until now.

The Beaver's engine hummed as he ratcheted up his airspeed toward Talkeetna, racing toward the early winter sunset.

Janet had called his cell to say Bob was stable, but they'd be staying another day or two in Anchorage. Jessie called to remind him about the Christmas brunch tomorrow morning, and Kreston seized the opportunity to let her know he wouldn't be back until then. He didn't elaborate, and when she bombarded him with questions, he pretended static and dropped the call. He knew the suspense would drive her insane.

He scanned his recent calls and texts, but nothing from Sadie. Then it hit him like a 747—they hadn't exchanged phone numbers. There hadn't been a need for it, yet he still cursed himself for not doing it.

"Talkeetna Traffic, DeHavilland N565TA, do you copy?"

"N565TA, Talkeetna. Go ahead."

"Incoming from Anchorage. ETA thirty minutes." His voice stayed steady despite his racing heart and what he was about to do. "Request permission to land."

"Copy that, N565TA," replied the Talkeetna tower. "Winds are calm with unlimited visibility. A Christmas miracle kind of day."

Kreston hoped so. The sun hung low over the Alaska Range, painting Denali's rugged face in shades of rose and gold. Kreston was savvy enough not to attempt night flying near these massifs without certification. He knew the terrain, but the eyes played tricks on you in the pitch black, no matter how much snow lit things up.

As usual, these past few days, his thoughts drifted to Sadie. Like how she'd taken charge after finding Ten Second Tess in the snow. He admired her cheerful demeanor in the early morning, and how she chatted with Tucker and Ten Second Tess like old friends, despite Tess never remembering her name.

And kissing her with every ounce of passion he possessed. She understood the part of him that worried about failing others. They were similar in that regard. Sadie was a kindred spirit...and soul mate material.

Kreston urged his plane to eat up the miles between him and the woman who'd become front and center in his life in such a brief time. In Manhattan, he'd chased success until it destroyed him. In Polar Creek, he'd chased redemption to make up for the destruction.

Chasing this woman was different. He wanted her to stay in his life and hadn't felt this way about anyone in a long time. Sadie was intelligent, funny, compassionate, and beautiful. He'd use every power of persuasion to convince her to stay.

Kreston landed in the soft winter twilight just as the sun dropped below the mountains. Good timing. He put his plane to bed next to a hangar and used his cell to call Denali Roadhouse for a shuttle. It was only half a mile away. If he had more energy, he'd walk. But it was cold, and he was worn out from all the flying.

On the way to the Roadhouse, Kreston asked the driver how business was today.

"Picked up a woman from Polar Creek and took her to the resort, but that's about it. We don't get many guests on Christmas Eve other than family reunion parties or locals who want a holiday getaway from Fairbanks and Anchorage."

"Was she, by any chance, a redhead?" asked Kreston.

"Come to think of it, yes." The driver pulled up to the front of the roadhouse. "And quite the beauty. Friend of yours?"

"Something like that." Kreston climbed out, his trusty emergency backpack over his shoulder. Inside were a change of clothes and a toothbrush—ready for whatever came his way.

The Denali Roadhouse glowed with warmth and Christmas lights as Kreston opened the tall wooden door and ambled in. He crossed the gleaming wood floors to stand before the check-in desk.

"Well, well, well. Look what the ravens dragged in," simpered Rochelle, greeting him.

"Hey Rochelle, fancy meeting you here." He smiled. "Been a long time. How are you doing?"

"Not too shabby. Looks like you're doing okay." Her eyes roved him. "Let's see. I have a hunch why you suddenly popped out of the blue. She's in the restaurant." Smirking, Rochelle pointed to his right.

Surprised at her incredible psychic ability, he swiveled his head toward the Eagle's Perch restaurant.

"Seriously? She told you about me?" His voice rose upon learning his worlds had collided—his ex and his...his what?

Current girlfriend, he decided once and for all.

She folded her arms. "I met your Sadie and talked to her."

"She's not my Sadie," he mumbled. "Not yet, anyway. Why were you both talking about me?" He shook his head, baffled.

*How do women talk about stuff like this right after meeting each other?*

Rochelle gave him a lopsided grin. "It was more like I asked her, since she'd just arrived from Polar Creek. Plus, I'm no dummy. She had a pouty, lovesick thing going on. I figured it probably had something to do with you."

"You make it sound like I chase every woman in Alaska." He tilted his head with bewildered interest. "And what did she say?"

Rochelle tipped her head toward The Perch. "Why don't you go ask her?"

"Okay, thanks. I don't know for what, but...thanks." He took a deep breath and headed inside the restaurant.

Rochelle hollered after him. "I wouldn't screw this up if I were you."

He halted for a fleeting moment, then continued inside the dimly lit but decorative restaurant. Candles flickered on the tables, and twinkling holiday lights created a cozy ambiance. A fire crackled in a hearth on one wall, giving off a familiar woodsy smell.

"There she is," he said under his breath, spotting an auburn-haired woman sitting in a booth with her back to him, firelight playing in her hair.

"That doesn't look like Arctic char to me," he drawled from behind her.

She whirled around, disbelief flickering across her face.

"Oh my God, Kreston!" she practically shrieked. She bolted from the booth and threw her arms around his neck. "I can't believe you're here."

"Couldn't let you go without saying goodbye," he whispered, eyeing people at other tables staring at them. He couldn't care less who stared. He was just happy to see her.

"How's Hardware Bob? I heard what happened." She backed up, motioning to the seat across from her. "Take a load off. Have you eaten?"

"Bob's stable but still in the Anchorage hospital for another day or two. And no, I haven't eaten." He wondered if she heard his gurgling stomach.

"Thank goodness. I felt bad that Lucky had to fly me, since you had to take Bob and Janet to Anchorage," she said. Just like Sadie to be concerned about everyone else.

"I didn't mind. It all worked out." He slid into the booth and removed his parka, setting it to the side. "Sorry I didn't talk to you before you left. I didn't mean for that to happen."

"Did you have another reason to fly to Talkeetna?" she asked in a tentative voice.

"No reason other than to see you."

Her expression softened as his words registered. "No one has ever come after me."

His eyes met hers. "I've never *gone* after anyone before."

"Why are you doing it now?"

There it was. His moment of truth: what he should have told her a thousand times in the last week if he hadn't been such a chickenshit.

"Well, for starters." He rested his forearms on the table. "It's the way you handle crisis with grace. How you get to the heart of what matters. The way you make Ten Second Tess feel valued, even though she forgets who the heck you are."

"Is that all?" Firelight glittered gold in her hair.

He wanted to do unmentionable things to her.

"You're the part of my life I didn't know was missing—until you arrived."

Her amber eyes sparkled. "Really? You aren't kidding me?"

Kreston sat back and folded his arms. "I don't kid about things like that."

A server appeared, and he greeted her. "I'll have your Halibut Olympia and mashed potatoes. And a hot buttered rum. It's Christmas Eve. Why not?" He shrugged at Sadie.

"You're right, why not? I'll have a rum, too," she told the server, who nodded and stepped away.

Kreston motioned at her half-eaten plate of salmon. "Are you done with that?" He had a slight headache after not eating all day. "If you don't mind. I'm starving."

"Sure. Help yourself." She pushed her plate toward him.

"All I had today was a stale granola bar." He gratefully accepted her leftovers and devoured them.

"Don't forget to save room for your halibut," she said, laughing.

"Not a problem." He dabbed at his mouth with a napkin and slid the empty plate to the edge of the table.

"About the part where you said something was missing from your life until I showed up in Polar Creek. Can you elaborate?" She gave him a close-mouthed smile.

"First, I'd like *you* to elaborate. Why did you take off like a meteor when I kissed you the night of the party?" He looked up at the ceiling, thinking. "Was it last night or the night before? I've lost track of time."

She traced the rim of her water glass. "I wrote you an email, then deleted it. How do you explain you're terrified of wanting someone because you're afraid of taking a risk and being hurt again?"

"Sadie, I think we've reached a point where you can confide in me. At least, I hope we have. Once it goes in here..." he pointed to his ear. "It stays in lock-up without a key."

"There's the other part of the equation." She flicked her eyes at him. "Can I trust you?"

"Does a moose drop nuggets?" He threw his arms up. "Yes, you can trust me. You shouldn't even have to ask. It's a given." So, this was her issue. He berated himself for not thinking of it.

She laughed at his predictable moose comment and rested her forearms on the table.

"I have a corner office and a six-figure salary, with a stellar reputation for what I do. And I hate it." She looked at him directly. "Hate managing other people's screw-ups. Hate watching celebrities destroy others' lives along with their own and then expect me to make their problems vanish, like I'm David Copperfield."

"And now?" he asked. "Let me guess. You're wondering if you climbed the wrong mountain."

"Maybe not the wrong mountain, but I got lost on the one I climbed." She looked up at him. "How did you walk away from everything you worked so hard for?"

"I crashed and burned. There was no other choice." He gave her a wry smile. "Best thing that ever happened to me. Learned the difference between success and fulfillment."

A server set down Kreston's halibut and the two cups of hot beverages. Soft Christmas music in the background played as he dug into his mashed potatoes and halibut, then sipped his hot buttered rum. He closed his eyes and leaned back.

"Ah, so good, so good."

She studied him, her chin resting on her hand. "You still eat like a Manhattan executive. Perfect manners. Precise, elegant movements."

He snorted. "Elegant? You analyze people like you work in public relations or something," he teased. "Tell me, why did you choose PR work?"

"I thought I could do good for people. And I did, as I worked my way up the reputation ladder." She sipped her rum. "Now, all I do is make problems disappear and repair images for the rich and famous. Mostly professional athletes who can do no wrong."

She gave him a plaintive look. "Is that what you did? Choose Polar Creek?"

"Polar Creek chose me. Like it chose Tucker, Jessie, and the others." He reached across the table to hold her hand. "Like it's chosen you, if you're brave enough to let it."

"I can't just abandon my life, Kreston—" she yanked her hand away, shaking her head.

He interrupted. "I'm not suggesting you do. But what if you come back with me to Polar Creek and stay through New Year's? See if what we have so far is worth pursuing?"

Her eyes met his, vulnerable and searching. "What do we have so far?"

"Here's the thing. You're the first woman I've wanted to spend time with since forever...like treading solid ground after years of tiptoeing on ice." He hesitated. "Do you want to spend time with me, too?"

She swallowed, her gaze locked on his. "That's all I want to do."

Sadie ignited the simmering flame that had flickered in his heart from day one.

"Neither of us is getting any younger. We're both pushing forty. Let's stop wasting time and being afraid to love again," Kreston said softly. "You don't have to stay forever. Just one more week. The worst that could happen is we find we aren't compatible. Then we go our separate ways."

"I'm scared," she whispered. "Scared of wanting this with you."

"Look, Sadie, I'm not the cheating kind. I won't cheat on you, if that's what's holding you back. I would never do that."

She leaned back and let out a long exhale. "All right. You talked me into it. We'll test-drive each other for another week."

"See? That wasn't so hard, was it?" he chirped, happy as hell he'd convinced her.

She lowered her chin, eyeing him the way a lion locks onto a zebra. "I have a sudden desire to make out with you. Care to join me in my room? I have a cozy hot tub for two."

He hadn't expected that little zinger to come flying out of her mouth...but he wanted to do a heck of a lot more than just make out. His arm shot across the table like a bullet.

"Twist it. Go ahead, twist hard."

She laughed. "Figured you'd be onboard with it, Captain Collins. Let's go." She charged the meal to her room, then stood, waiting.

He pointed at her. "I'm paying for my halibut dinner."

"No, you aren't. Already took care of it." She smirked and led the way from the restaurant.

Relieved that he'd accomplished what he'd set out to do in coming here, he followed her like a lovesick puppy across the lobby.

She stopped and turned around. "If I agree to return with you to Polar Creek, then I want you to show me why you chose to live in Alaska."

"Agreed." He hoped her green-lighting the possibility of staying might extend beyond New Year's. He would do his best to convince her. He'd get Jessie and the rest of the town to help him.

It occurred to him the bravest thing wasn't running from a broken past; it was running toward a favorable future.

# Chapter 22

*Sadie*

Rochelle gave Sadie a thumbs-up in an all-systems-go gesture as Sadie and Kreston passed the front desk on their way to the elevator.

Once on the third floor, the historic wooden floor creaked as they ambled along the hallway to Sadie's room. Her hand trembled as she turned her room key, hyperaware of Kreston's presence behind her. Inside, her room glowed with the warm light she'd left on. Out her window, the northern lights danced in the night sky.

"I better call Lucky. Let him know I won't be back tonight." Kreston tapped his phone speaker for Sadie's benefit. "Let's see if he has reception."

Thankfully, the call went through, and Lucky's voice burst through the speaker.

"Well, Jesus, Mary, and Joseph!" Lucky's thick brogue suggested multiple Jamesons had been involved. "If it isn't our wandering mayor. And where might you be this fine evening?" It sounded like he was at the Crooked Spoon, and the whole town was partying down.

"Overnighting in Talkeetna at Denali Roadhouse. Didn't want you to worry." Kreston raised his phone and stage-whispered to Sadie, "Wait for it, wait for it..."

As expected, Lucky whooped and hollered, then announced to his party cohorts, "Mayor Collins is spending Christmas Eve in Talkeetna!"

Amid the uproar of whoops and hollers, Lucky yelled into the phone, "Lemme guess—you're with a certain copper-haired lass who's finally come to her senses? Or perhaps you've both come to your senses?"

"You could say that," Kreston answered, his eyes meeting Sadie's with such intensity it made her breath catch. She remembered his same look when they kissed the night before.

The continuing explosion of cheers from his phone nearly deafened them, and both burst out laughing. Sadie secretly loved it.

"Aloha! Welcome to the romance of the century!" Aloha's voice carried clearly over the chaos, and Sadie heard a deck of cards shuffle.

"It's about time!" Jessie's voice overrode everyone else's congratulatory remarks.

"We knew it!" gushed the Gossip Trio in unison.

"Mayor Collins, we love you!" Ten Second Tess chimed in. "Come home and kiss under the mistletoe! I forgot where I put it, but it'll turn up, you know, like a turnip?" She laughed at her own pun.

Lucky howled, "Kreston, your dogs miss you!"

"Mayor Collins has dogs?" Ten Second Tess piped up.

"Got to go now. Merry Christmas to everyone! See you tomorrow," Kreston hollered into the phone.

"Merry Christmas!" yelled Sadie, then Kreston ended the call.

"They're happy about our news. Come here, Seattle." Kreston waggled his finger at her. "Let's get a selfie with the northern lights."

She snuggled into him as he held his phone out, positioning it to capture them against the light show out the window.

"Look, red and green for Christmas Eve!" Sadie whispered as Kreston pulled her in tight and kissed her lightly on the lips.

She hungered for more, but they had all night. Right now, she reveled in the fact he'd come after her. Actions speak louder than words. Even if he said nothing the rest of the night, she wouldn't care. The fact he was here spoke volumes.

She didn't need his words.

Kreston powered down his phone and plugged it in. "How about a soak? Except I don't have my swimsuit."

"I do." She wasn't yet comfortable to strip naked in front of him. She was shy and had to ease into it.

"I have an extra pair of boxers." He unzipped his small backpack.

She didn't know whether to be relieved or what. All they'd done until now was kiss.

"Whatever makes *you* comfortable. See you in the hot tub." Sadie snatched the bikini she'd packed for hot tubbing. On the way into the bathroom to change, she reveled in how quickly things had changed on this holiday trip to Alaska.

*Who would have thought I'd be spending Christmas with an Alaskan bush pilot and mayor of a town instead of the person I'd intended to marry?*

Sadie wrapped herself in the terrycloth robe she'd found hanging on the bathroom door, then opened the sliding glass door leading to the cedar deck and the two-person hot tub. The chill hit her skin, goose-bumping it. She scurried over, tossed off the bathrobe, and climbed in. She lowered herself into the frothing water across from Kreston, who was enjoying his soak with closed eyes.

He opened them when her toes touched him underwater. "Look up."

Sadie's breath caught at the emerald ribbons twisting around bursts of red and purple above them. She luxuriated in the hot water, every sense on hyper-drive as the steam rose and vaporized. The contrast between the hot tub's warmth and the crisp December air, along with the sight of a half-naked Kreston, raised goosebumps on her exposed shoulders.

It was exhilarating.

Christmas carols drifted up from the Roadhouse's main deck, accompanied by laughter and the clink of glasses. Below them, people clustered around a large gas-fired deck heater, talking and laughing.

"I'm the luckiest woman in the world right now," she murmured, rubbing her foot up and down his leg.

Kreston smiled in response and sat up, lifting the champagne bottle from a table next to him. He poured the bubbly into two plastic flutes with measured precision, his graceful movements shooting straight to her core, turning her on. She loved the perfect fusion of East Coast refinement and Alaskan ruggedness, setting him in a unique class all his own.

He offered her the champagne, and she leaned forward to accept it, grateful for his companionship on this Christmas Eve.

"Thank you. You're so classy," she teased.

"To second chances." Kreston tapped her glass as steam swirled between them like a happy dream.

"And being brave enough to take them," she added, her body tingling with the anticipation of what would unfold tonight. "I appreciate your understanding of my job situation. It's like we're kindred spirits."

His brows winged up, and he chortled. "I've been thinking the same thing. Tell me what happened—with you and—what's his name?"

"Clayton." She traced the rim of her glass. "I spent so much time and energy managing other people's situations, I ignored my own life. With Clayton, it was easy to be co-dependent. I relied on him to manage our relationship. He controlled all of it. All of me. And the worst part was, I let him."

She furrowed her brow. "Didn't realize it until I got to Alaska. When he texted, and I knew he'd been cheating, I finally opened my eyes to see things for what they really were."

"Must have ripped you in half. I can't imagine the hurt." He shook his head.

Her eyes watered. "I feel like a fool, allowing him to control me like that."

He reached for her hand and squeezed it. "You're anything but a fool. You just needed to distance yourself from the situation, that's all." He sipped, his Adam's apple bobbing as he swallowed. She found it erotic, shooting to her core along with everything else about him.

Sadie downed her champagne, loving the buzz and warmth that spread through her. She thrust out her empty glass. "When I caught Clayton cheating, I texted him it was over. But he didn't even fight for us—instead, he cast me aside like yesterday's trash. But you…" she trailed off, resisting the impulse to fling herself into Kreston's arms.

"You came after me, and you hardly know me."

Kreston refilled her glass. "Because you're worth pursuing. Your ex is a mother-effing bonehead." He set the bottle on the table and moved toward her. He brushed back a tendril from her cheek, leaving trails of hot lava on her skin.

Sadie emptied her glass, and he took it from her and set it on the table. The Aurora reflected in his eyes, each color mirroring her emotions: hope, desire, and what she was finally brave enough to admit.

That she loved him.

# Chapter 23

K*reston*

"Are you still scared?" His voice was quiet as he sensed her tension.

"Terrified." Sadie appeared to relax when his hand found her bare waist under the water.

"Me too, but it's okay," he confessed. "The best things in life should scare us a little."

His lips found hers and he nipped them, no longer able to hold himself back. The heat from his kiss could easily ignite and set them on fire. Their first kiss had been tentative. This one was nothing like that. Instead, this kiss was cast-iron certainty on both their parts.

Kreston cradled her face with the same gentle confidence as he approached everything. His fingers smoothed over her skin, exploring the map of her to memorize. He slid his lips down the side of her neck, and she tilted her head back, allowing him to have anything he wanted. He nibbled his way back to her lips for another passionate tongue exchange.

When he lifted off, Sadie licked her lips. "Thanks for the taste of extra rum. The halibut tasted good, too."

Kreston laughed. "It's Alaskan breath. Fish and booze. The perfect combo. And yours tastes sweet from the salmon."

"Let's move this operation inside, where it's dry and warm, shall we?"

He loved this suggestion, planning to ravish her the first chance he got. He'd show her a million-and-one reasons she should stay. He'd surrender himself completely and unconditionally. He didn't want to do all the taking...he prided himself as a giver.

Kreston stepped out and wrapped himself in another white terrycloth robe he'd found in her closet. He lifted hers from a deck chair and stood behind her, holding it open when she stepped out. He quickly wrapped it around her and spun her around to face him.

He gave her a light kiss, then spoke against her lips, "It's mother-effing cold out here. Let's get inside."

They beelined for the sliding glass doors, then Sadie made for the bathroom. "I have to shower to rinse off these hot tub chemicals."

When he removed his robe, her eyes froze on his bare-chested physique. He suppressed a laugh, loving the amazed look on her face. He didn't know what was going on in that head of hers, though, so he checked in.

"Everything okay?"

"Better than okay. Be out in a minute." She hurried into the spacious bathroom and closed the door.

The shower turned on, and Kreston impulsively stripped off his drenched boxers and opened the bathroom door. He slid the curtain aside and nearly passed out upon seeing her slick, naked body. Her hands busily shampooed the hair piled on her head, and his eyes immediately went to her sizeable breasts, standing at attention in a 'hello, big boy' greeting.

"Mind if I join you?" Kreston stepped in, and the surprise on her face was priceless.

"Do I have a choice?" she sputtered through the water, spraying her face.

"Thought you might like your back washed." He waggled his brows. "Plus, I believe in conserving water, since I also needed a shower."

She sputtered. "You're a smooth-talking politician, aren't you, Mayor Collins?"

Kreston was anything but in his mayor mode at the moment. Right now, he was a man on a different mission. He soaped a washcloth and drifted it up and down Sadie's back, loving her little squeaks and moans.

"This is absolute heaven," she croaked out, dropping her head back.

He slid his lips along her throat while massaging her skin with the soapy washcloth. Kreston worked his way down each leg, then pressed himself to her back and reached around her waist to massage the front of her. He took his time massaging each breast, treating them with reverence.

"You know how to charm a girl." She twisted to face him. She took the washcloth from his hand and did the same for him. He turned his back to her, and she rubbed the washcloth over his soapy skin, fingering his back muscles with her other hand.

"This is fun," he murmured, turning to face her.

She moved the washcloth around his chest and stomach but stopped short of going lower. He sensed she was shy about their being naked together, so he took her in his arms and drew her under the pelting water. "Have you ever been kissed in the shower? I mean, really, truly kissed?"

She gazed up at him, shaking her head. "My ex never enjoyed showering together."

"Well, I do." He grabbed hold of her and kissed her with as much passion as he could summon, which wasn't difficult since Little Kreston stood straight up, saluting the two of them.

She looked smitten when he released her, encouraging him on his quest to make love to her like no other man ever had. The mention of her ex had caught him off guard. He knew then she wasn't completely over that loser, and resolved to help her forget him.

"I can't believe how long I've missed out on this." She turned off the spray and motioned for him to step out. "After you, Mister Water Conservation."

Before she could reach for a towel, he offered her a neatly folded one.

"Thanks, Mayor Collins."

He loved tending to her needs. But then, that's who he was. The last thing he expected was to find someone like Sadie in Polar Creek—much less to fall for her—and now they were naked together. Today was a crucial turning point in this relationship. He wanted, no, *needed* this relationship to have staying power.

He thought for a moment, hesitating. "Sadie, are you sure about all this? With me, I mean? I don't want you to do anything you aren't comfortable doing."

She poked her head out of the curtain, beaming at him. "You mean like stepping naked into the shower with me? It's a little too late for that, buddy."

Kreston glimpsed her heart-shaped derriere, and Little Kreston noticed it, too. He cleared his throat and swallowed. "Like I said, I believe in conserving water."

She snorted. "As if you need to conserve water in Alaska. Good grief, you guys are swimming in water up here with millions of lakes and rivers. Not to mention an endless snowpack like a frozen Pacific Ocean."

Sadie's relaxed attitude told him everything he needed to know: all systems were a go for launch. He chuckled to himself and stepped out of the steam-filled bathroom, closing the door behind him.

# Chapter 24

*Sadie*

S adie dried herself off and put her robe back on. She blow-dried her hair and flirted with the idea of applying make-up. Then she remembered Kreston had seen her without make-up for the better part of a week.

She was still shy with him. His intense testosterone had her pheromones jumbled together as if on the frappe setting of a blender.

When she opened the door, she found him resting on his back with his eyes closed on the queen bed, his feet hanging over the end.

She crawled onto the bed and snuggled into him. "Before we—you know, do anything...can we talk first?"

He rolled to his side and adjusted himself, trying not to let Little Kreston poke her. "Sure. What's on your mind?"

Sadie traced idle patterns on his bare chest. "The worst part wasn't the cheating. It was how disposable I felt. Four years together, and he couldn't even send his texts to the right woman. What kind of bonehead gets blindsided by her own fiancé?"

"Hey, don't belittle yourself. Do me a favor." Kreston's voice was gentle but firm. "Whenever you feel sad about your cheating ex, remember that the woman who is dating him thinks she's found someone special. That should give you some sense of comfort. And chances are, he'll cheat on her, too. Once a cheater, always a cheater."

Sadie laughed. "Haven't thought of it that way. You're absolutely right."

"Besides." His hand rested on her waist. "His douchey move led you to me."

She gave him an apologetic look. "I didn't apologize for my behavior when I first arrived in Polar Creek. I was hurt, so I lashed out at anyone who got in my way. I'm so sorry."

He cupped her cheek. "Apology accepted, but unnecessary. I know what it's like to be hurt and take it out on everyone except the one who caused it. I get it."

"I knew there was a reason I liked you." She propped herself up on an elbow. "Want to know the truth? The moment you opened Lucky's plane door that first day, I thought you were the hottest thing since Jessie's five-alarm moose chili."

His laugh rumbled from his chest. "Her moose chili gave Tucker the screaming meemies for three days. He couldn't leave his bathroom." His expression turned serious. "Thanks for the hot comment. I thought the same thing about you."

"Okay, true confession. All the way to Polar Creek in your truck that first night, you sent my heart rate to dangerous levels. Then, during the outhouse race, I saw how you laughed at yourself. And when you told me about leaving your big city life behind, well..." She traced his jaw. "I admire the man you've become. I was definitely falling. But when you showed up at my hotel room in your tuxedo...whoa..." She blew out air.

"So that clinched it for you?"

"Absolutely."

"I wish you would have spoken up. Given me some kind of sign instead of running away."

Sadie guffawed. "Seriously? And what would I have said? Gee, Mayor Collins, I think you are mother-effing hot, and I want to jump your bones? And, oh, by the way, I've fallen head over heels for you."

"Yes, you should have said all that. Every word." He said it like he was dead serious.

"Right. Then you would have thought you had a horny, big-city snob on your hands."

He laughed outright. "No, but if you would have said something, it would have sped things up."

"I couldn't. I was so confused. I wanted to hurt my ex, but I didn't want to use you as a rebound."

His fingers stilled on her back. "Is that what this is? A rebound?"

"No! Not at all." She met his eyes firmly. "A rebound is running from pain. This is running toward...you. What shocks me is how right it feels."

He eased into a smile. "Hell, I fell for you even before you landed in Lucky's plane, when he said he had a Christmas present for me."

"Get out of town! You did not."

"Uh-huh, ask Lucky."

She laughed into his chest. "We're quite a pair. The Wall Street refugee and the public relations expert, in the middle of nowhere, Alaska. I'm glad the blizzard happened, and I didn't go straight home."

"Speaking of home..." He grew serious. "You say you detest your job. Do you plan to go back to it?"

She'd expected him to ask this. "I've been thinking about that very thing. But I've also been thinking about other things."

"Like what?" His touch ratcheted up her want of him.

She smiled against his skin. "These small Alaskan towns have such incredible stories. Polar Creek alone—you've got Lucky's tall tales about his close calls with The Beave, Ten Second Tess greeting people for the first time every ten minutes, and a mayor who sings Helen Reddy songs."

"That was a one-time performance under duress," he corrected her.

She ran her finger across his lips. "You're a talented singer."

A knock at the door made them both jump.

"Who is it?" Sadie called out in a cheerful voice.

Rochelle's muffled voice sounded through the door. "Lucky O'Hara is on the landline downstairs—something about the whole town wanting to sing Christmas carols to you through the speakerphone?"

Kreston and Sadie burst out laughing. "Tell them we're..."

"Sleeping!" they said in unison.

"Right, 'sleeping.'" Rochelle's air quotes were audible. "I'll tell him you're indisposed. Merry Christmas, you two!"

"Merry Christmas!" they chorused, laughing.

As Rochelle's footsteps faded away, Kreston rolled onto his back with his forearm over his face. "Lucky must be shitfaced."

"Will be fun seeing everyone's hangovers tomorrow morning," said Sadie. "By the way, your ex-girlfriend Rochelle is nice. Too bad you let her go." She was testing him.

"Yeah, what a shame," he said dismissively, pulling her into him. "Come here, you beauty. And lose this thing." He tugged on her robe, and she wriggled out of it.

"Oh, God," he whispered with a fast intake of breath as he gazed at her.

Through the open curtains, lazy snowflakes drifted past the window, adding to the magic of Sadie's perfect Christmas Eve.

"I can't believe I have you all to myself," she breathed, sliding next to him. "You need to lose these." She tapped his boxers, and he had them off so fast she laughed.

"Do you have protection?" she asked.

"Yep," he responded, reaching for a packet on the bedside table.

Sadie yielded her trust, and they relaxed into each other with tender touches and kissing. He was a good kisser, and she didn't want him to stop. She loved the intimacy, his warmth, the stubble on his chin.

Her need quickly fired up, waving through her like a furnace. Now that she had Kreston Collins in her arms, she couldn't get enough of him. Truth be told, she'd wanted this ever since he'd kissed her at the holiday party. No denying him now. She was too far gone. She had to have him, and she sensed he felt the same by the way his breathing sped up.

"You're trembling," he whispered against her neck.

"But in a good way," she assured him, aching for more of his touch.

Their connection deepened with each shared breath, each tender caress. He traced the curve of her spine like charting a beloved flight path, while she mapped the strength in his shoulders that had flown through myriads of storms. As they explored one another and learned each other's wants and desires, Sadie was helpless to throttle back the dizzying current speeding through her.

Their mouths continued the sensuous rhythm of giving and taking, the way she loved kissing. He broke the kiss to roam his lips around her shoulders and chest. She arched to offer him greater access, and he didn't hesitate to take advantage of it.

He sheathed himself, then moved over her and threaded his fingers with hers to claim her. Their hands squeezed together as he entered her, their bodies joined, deepening every emotion and fantasy she'd ever had about him.

There was no going back after this. No way. Her breath snagged on the sudden rush of air she sucked in when he pushed in all the way and began moving.

"Oh, Kreston!" He launched her into euphoria as mindless pleasure devoured her. She floated off to who knows where. She loved him, but something kept her from telling him, despite his sending her off to orbit the Big Dipper.

Soon after, he stiffened and shuddered, following her to release. Fighting for breath, Kreston dropped his forehead to hers, and they clung to each other—bodies joined and minds blurred. Their connection felt whole and complete.

Sadie cradled Kreston's face and kissed him lightly before he rolled onto his back, panting. The Aurora had gone to sleep, allowing the moon to take over. Moonbeams caressed Kreston's handsome face as she studied him.

"I never expected to find this," she whispered, laying her head on his chest, where his heartbeat gradually slowed beneath her fingertips.

"Me neither," he replied. "This was the last thing I expected."

"You've been so busy taking care of everyone else that you neglected your own heart," she whispered.

"I'm taking care of it now." His fingers wandered through her hair. "Being with you is amazing. I don't know how to explain it—"

"Like finding a piece of yourself you didn't know was missing?" she finished for him.

"Exactly." He pulled her closer, pressing a kiss to her temple.

They lay in comfortable silence, listening to the distant sounds of Christmas music drifting up from below. She felt satiated and newly awakened, as if every nerve ending was renewed by his touch.

"What are you thinking?" he asked.

"That I've never felt so cherished." She propped herself up to look at him. "Like I matter for who I am, not what I can do or how I can fix people's lives."

"You'll never need to prove yourself with me." His smile was tender in the shifting light. "You've already fixed mine."

His words made her soul sing. "I can't wait to see everyone tomorrow morning." She truly meant it. She missed Jessie, Aloha, and Ten Second Tess. And Lucky. And Tucker...and the rest.

"It'll be interesting, to say the least." He yawned. "We'd better get some sleep."

"Great idea." After visiting the bathroom, they crawled under the crisp sheet and thick comforter.

This was pure heaven.

With Kreston's arm around her, Sadie felt a sense of peace she hadn't felt in forever, and she drifted off to a deep, restful sleep, feeling safe and protected.

She wanted to stay this way forever.

# Chapter 25

reston

Kreston woke to the sunrise painting Mount Denali in shades of rose gold. Beside him, Sadie stirred, copper hair catching the early light. His heart did that thing it had done ever since she'd arrived in Polar Creek—a skip and a tumble that made him realize how empty his carefully ordered life had been before meeting her.

"Merry Christmas," he murmured.

Her eyes fluttered open, the remarkable amber-gold that skipped his heart. "Merry Christmas. It's so bright in here." Her forearm covered her eyes.

He kissed her before she could say more.

"Morning breath!" she protested against his lips.

"Don't care." He kissed her again. "Never cared less about anything in my life."

Denali dominated their window view as they dressed, its jagged morning shadows clear in the crystallized air outside. These were perfect flight conditions, and Kreston couldn't wait to take her up in his plane. Flying fed his soul, like it did as the mayor, running the hotel, and all the other responsibilities he'd piled on to avoid his lonely heart.

No more. Not with Sadie here.

Kreston moved away from the window and got dressed. "Should be a smooth flight to Polar Creek. We'd better get going, though. Weather in the Alaska Range can change in a nanosecond."

Sadie pressed her palm to the window glass like a child seeing snow for the first time.

Kreston made a sudden decision to give her the best Christmas present ever. "I have a surprise for you, but you'll have to wait and see what it is."

"Ooh, what?" She slid her arms around his neck. "You've already given me the best Christmas present I could ever want. You standing here with me, like this."

He kissed her lightly. "There's more to come. Hurry and dress."

Kreston looked forward to the day's celebration back in Polar Creek. By now, Jessie would have her delectable rolls in the oven, and Tucker would be at his usual table, sketching and sipping coffee. Ten Second Tess would be bouncing around like an excited child, wanting to open Christmas presents every ten minutes. He'd only been away from Polar Creek for a day, and already he missed it.

But first, he wanted to impress Sadie with an unforgettable flight experience. He also wanted her to feel safe with his piloting skills.

The hotel shuttle dropped them off at the Talkeetna Airport, and Kreston's DeHavilland Beaver sat waiting, its red and blue paint gleaming in the morning sun. He ran through his pre-flight checks, his mind drifting to how different this was from their first meeting with her displeased arrival in Lucky's plane. And those ridiculous designer boots. And the way she'd looked at him like he was the most annoying person she'd ever met.

"Your plane's colors are prettier than Lucky's," Sadie observed, running a hand along the fuselage.

"Don't tell him that. He named every red stripe on his plane. Says it's for the women he's known." Kreston mimicked commercial pilot announcements. "Climb aboard and welcome to Polar Creek Airlines, the only way to fly."

After loading his backpack and Sadie's bags into the cargo hold, he made sure her passenger door was secure. He climbed into his seat and started the engine. It was cold, so it took a try or two for the engine to kick in and turn the propellor.

Kreston handed Sadie her headset and placed his over his ears. He activated the mics so they could easily talk to each other through the plane noise. After Talkeetna cleared him for takeoff, he taxied to the end of the runway and positioned the plane. The runway had been plowed, so he lifted the hydraulic skis on his landing gear, letting the wheels control the takeoff.

"Power up your phone," he instructed Sadie, changing the radio frequency. "Talkeetna, this is DeHavilland N565TA, do you copy?"

"Yes, copy. N565TA, go ahead."

"Request takeoff for Polar Creek, including a flightseeing trip around the mountain. Over."

"N565TA, you're clear. Should be a spectacular view. Merry Christmas," a woman replied.

"Merry Christmas, N565TA clear." He flashed a sideways glance at his gorgeous passenger.

Sadie's eyes grew to saucers. "Did you mean Denali? We're flying around Denali? Oh, my God!" If it weren't for her seat belt, she would have jumped up and down in her seat.

Kreston chortled as he throttled up. He lifted the plane and broke free of the ground, loving how it handled on this beautiful Christmas day. In fifteen minutes, they were over the Ruth Glacier, elongated in striated ribbons of dark gray, blue, and white, like the world's largest toboggan run.

"This is Ruth Glacier, where I shuttle climbers in the summer. She's thirty-five miles long," he explained into his mic.

Sadie's jaw dropped. "There. Are. No. Words." Her look of incredulity was what he'd been aiming for. He had that same look when Lucky had flown him through here for the first time.

"I know." He lifted the cardboard cup of coffee they'd each poured themselves in the hotel lobby.

The flight so far had been smooth, except for the occasional wind gusting through the saddles between the tall peaks. He pointed down, and Sadie's gaze darted to the jagged blue crevasses in the heart of the glacier, their edges sharp and glittering in the sunlight. As they flew deeper into the Alaska Range, he pointed out the landmarks.

Kreston stole sidelong glances at Sadie as she took in the majestic, rugged peaks crowned in white, where gleaming cerulean glaciers carved their way through U-shaped valleys. Then, as if by magic, the mighty Denali made her grand entrance. Kreston had always found it hard to believe land could rise that high from the earth. The immensity and majesty of this mountain never ceased to amaze him.

"Oh my God, Kreston, look!" Tears pooled, and she swiped at her eyes. She turned to see him smiling at her.

"That's how I felt when I saw Denali for the first time." He pointed. "We're entering The Great Gorge at thirty-two hundred feet."

"This is incredible," she murmured.

Buttressed on either side by solid granite cliffs, The Great Gorge always reminded Kreston of a stairway to heaven, each proud landform outdoing the last, the grand entrance leading to Denali.

Kreston tracked the aircraft to the right and pointed to a towering metallic-looking cliff on the western side of the Gorge. "There's Moose's Tooth. Denali is a system of mountains all blended into one enormous mass of granite and ice."

He watched Sadie's face as she took it all in, her sharp intake of breath soaring his heart higher than the plane. He loved showing this to people for the first time. He loved showing it to *her.*

"I would land you on the Ruth Glacier, but we don't have time."

Her eyes widened in alarm. "I'm loving this, but you don't have to land on the glacier."

Kreston sensed her trepidation and remembered she was still new to all this. He reminded himself to expose her to more of Alaska in baby steps. He didn't want her to fear Alaska, but to love it as he did.

He banked the plane to fly through a low saddle to come out on the western side, careful not to fly too close to Denali, yet close enough to see the intricate patterns of steep rock jutting up almost to the troposphere. Wispy clouds hugged it as he flew higher so Sadie could look down on the summit.

"Merry Christmas, Sadie Foster." He aimed for as sexy of a tone as he could muster.

The look she gave him was priceless. "This is like orbiting the moon," she whispered, gazing out the windshield.

He carefully guided the plane around the mountain, showing Sadie the dramatic plays of light and shadow across ancient ice. Every crevasse told a story, and every jagged peak held secrets neither of them would ever know.

"Talkeetna to Ruth Glacier is our summer taxi route," he explained. "Dropping off climbers to conquer this beast."

"Do they always reach the summit?"

"Many do. Some succumb to altitude sickness and have to retreat. Most learn respect for the elements Denali throws at them," he explained.

Kreston realized something profound: he'd spent years showing people Alaska's beauty, but this was the first time he'd shared it with someone special, like Sadie. He banked the plane to set his course for Polar Creek. Twenty minutes and one lesser peak later, Polar Creek's airstrip emerged after flying over a lesser peak. Kreston switched to the local radio frequency. "Lucky, you copy? Bring my truck to the airstrip."

"Well, if it isn't the happy lovebird wanderers!" Lucky's brogue came into his headphones. "The whole town's waiting. And by waiting, I mean Jessie's baking enough for three Christmases. The Gossip Trio is already planning your wedding, and Ten Second Tess has switched the hotel decorations around so none of it makes sense."

"Copy that," replied Kreston, exchanging smiles with Sadie.

"It'll be bouncy like the first time you landed here, but don't worry, it's normal." He reduced his airspeed, set the small wing flaps, and lowered the skis to land on fresh snow on top of the hard snowpack. The skis touched down, and the plane jostled. Kreston's side-eye caught Sadie gripping her seat. He also noticed her chest jiggling, and he snapped his gaze forward. Now wasn't the time for Little Kreston to stand up and wave a Merry Christmas.

Kreston brought the plane to a halt next to their hangar, and the propellor stopped when he cut the engine. In the sudden quiet, he impulsively leaned toward Sadie, waggling his finger.

She leaned toward him. "What?"

He grasped her face with one hand and laid a kiss on her. "Welcome back, Sadie Foster."

"I can't wait!" she said when he lifted away. She was like a little kid on Christmas morning.

*Wait a minute, it* is *Christmas morning!* They climbed out and Kreston unloaded the cargo hold, hefting their gear into the back of his truck.

Lucky hopped out of the driver's seat. "Our prodigal mayor and the lovely Miss Sadie returns!" he announced, pulling both into a group bear hug. "Janet called. Bob has a new stent and a second chance. They'll be home for New Year's." He backed up, looking at them. "Seems like everyone's getting second chances lately."

"Good to see you, Lucky." Sadie patted his arm.

"Glad you're back, lass." Lucky pointed his thumb at Kreston. "This guy was beside himself yesterday after you'd gone."

"Really?" She flashed Kreston a look that melted him into a lovesick puddle.

Lucky climbed into the back seat, and Sadie hopped into the front passenger seat. Kreston cranked the engine, and they were on their way to town.

Kreston peered into the rearview mirror. "Hungover today? Sounded like you had a good time last night."

Lucky chuckled. "It was a wild night, for sure. Not too bad, though. Jessie cured it with Bailey's and coffee this morning."

Walking into Crooked Spoon felt like entering a holiday in Whoville. Jessie and the others had transformed the space into a winter wonderland. Prime rib and hot rolls sent rich aromas through the air. Halibut Olympia gleamed with a perfect garnish, and three different preparations of salmon—including Jessie's famous salmon cheese balls, raved about by the entire town—covered the buffet tables.

"Aloha! Welcome back, Sadie!" Aloha announced, holding a plate of cookies. "About time you two got together. Get in here and nibble on a cookie."

The wave of welcome that hit them was pure Polar Creek chaos. Henrietta, who'd taught Kreston her secret sourdough rolls and bread recipes, pressed a warm roll into his hand. "About time you found someone who can settle you down." She gave him a toothy grin.

Kreston knew he would hear this same thing repeatedly throughout the day. And probably for many days afterwards. But now he didn't mind.

Tucker set down an artistically arranged fruit platter and placed a hand on Kreston's shoulder. "Love requires both precision and abandon. You've mastered precision, my friend. Now it's time for the abandon."

Sadie squeezed his hand, and his chest swelled. He'd organized so many town events, managed so many celebrations, always been the capable leader everyone counted on. But watching Sadie move through the crowd—accepting cooking tips from Henrietta and the two Marthas, listening to Tucker's philosophy about Christmas cookies, and helping Ten Second Tess remember which plate was hers—made him feel complete.

"You know," Lucky sidled up to Kreston. "I remember when you first landed here. All Wall Street polish and broken dreams. You rebuilt your life by running this town. But in all that, I've not seen you look at spreadsheets the way you look at her." He nodded toward Sadie.

"Spreadsheets are easier," joked Kreston.

"And as warm as a polar bear's toenails." Lucky's grin softened. "She'd be good for you."

Kreston laughed. "Thanks, my friend. She's agreed to stay until New Year's. Beyond that, I can't say. Asking her to give up everything is a big ask." He winked at his buddy. "But if you and the rest of Polar Creek can convince her to stay even longer, I wouldn't object."

Lucky winked back. "We'll be up to the challenge, don't worry." He swaggered over to Aloha's cookie plate and popped one in his mouth.

Kreston moved up behind Sadie, placing his hand on her lower back. "So glad you're here," he breathed into her ear.

She twisted into him. "So am I."

# Chapter 26

S*adie*

Sadie had never experienced anything like the wall of welcome that hit her when she walked into the Crooked Spoon. In Seattle, returning from business trips meant empty apartments and voicemails about client crises. She was lucky to get a hello when she walked into her corner office, let alone anything else. Here, she could barely move through the crowd of genuine hugs and joy-filled faces.

Jessie rushed up, enveloping her in a cinnamon-scented hug. "You came back to us. I knew you would!"

Tears pricked Sadie's eyes when Ten Second Tess planted herself in front of her. "I think I remember you. You're from Talkeetna." She extended her hand. "I'm Tess. Pleased to meet you. What's your name?"

Sadie considered it progress. This was the first time Tess had any semblance of remembering her, despite not remembering her name. The best Christmas present ever.

Tucker handed her a napkin-wrapped gift and nodded at her to open it. "For you, my dear."

She tore off the napkin to see a framed sketch of Main Street and the buildings surrounding Polar Creek...with one added detail: a couple kissing in the middle of the street, with Sadie in her stilettos and Kreston in his tux. Her heart stuttered as she swallowed Tucker in a hug.

"Thank you. I'll treasure it always," she said, her voice tremoring.

Aloha moved in with a plethora of leis draped on one arm, holding a deck of cards. "I'm so glad you're back. Jessie missed having you to help, and I missed having you to talk to. Tess couldn't figure out what was missing. We hoped you and Kreston would get together." She placed a silk lei around Sadie's neck. "I got these online, twenty leis for ten bucks."

Sadie fingered it. "Thanks, Aloha. I love it." Everyone treated her like she'd been gone for months. It was delightfully overwhelming, and she embraced it.

Jessie spread her arms. "Everyone! The annual Christmas brunch is ready. Dig in!"

Everyone stampeded to the long tables lining one wall and wrapping around the other in an extended "L." Sadie couldn't believe the staggering amount of food.

Kreston appeared at her side, noting her hung jaw expression. "Everyone contributes. It's easier to have the potluck here instead of across the street. Jessie does the prime rib and fish, and the rest of us contribute our specialty dishes."

"I'm starving, come on." Sadie led him by the hand to get into the long line.

Aloha rushed up. "Please sing us a song while we wait to get our food? Pretty please with unicorns on top?" Her puppy dog eyes were a hard sell. "We want to hear you both sing."

Sadie turned to Kreston. "Are you game?"

He shrugged. "I am if you are."

"Aloha, sneak up there and get me a roll," whispered Sadie, her stomach gurgling.

Aloha did her bidding as Sadie and Kreston moved up to the karaoke machine, still on the table from the night they served the Arctic char. While Kreston powered it on and tested the microphone, Sadie bit into the warm roll, closing her eyes.

"Mm, so good."

"Mind if I pick?" he asked as she chewed, dragging two bar stools over for them to sit on.

She swallowed and smiled. "Nope, go ahead." The more she looked at Kreston, the hotter he was, and the more she fell for him. She shoved away the notion of what would happen after New Year's.

One day at a time.

The introduction to "Silent Night" filled the room, and the crowd quieted as Kreston sang the first few notes. His baritone sent chills down Sadie's spine. She joined him in the second verse, singing harmony, loving how her voice blended with his. He was by far the better singer, but she could hold her own.

"Santa Claus is Coming to Town" followed, turning the restaurant into an upbeat celebration. Sadie and Kreston moved between the tables, sharing the microphone. By this time, most people had their food and were seated at the tables.

Tucker joined in, along with the Gossip Trio. Ten Second Tess changed the song when it was her turn, but no one cared. Like everything else in this crazy town, it was taken in stride. Back in Sadie's stiff world of social events, such chaos wouldn't be tolerated.

Here, it was normal.

"Time for presents!" Jessie announced. "For our mayor and his—his—what are you calling her?" Jessie stage-whispered to Kreston.

He replied, "My friend from Seattle."

Sadie glanced at him in surprise, and he darted his eyes at her, raising his hands in an "I don't know what to say" stance.

Sadie called out to Jessie. "Girlfriend. I'm his girlfriend."

Kreston beamed at her, nodding his approval.

"Alrighty, then. First, our mayor's esteemed girlfriend," declared Jessie, producing a large, wrapped package and handing it to Sadie with a flourish and much ceremony.

Sadie opened it to find a pair of white bulbous bunny boots—practical and totally unglamorous, but perfectly Alaskan. In her old life, she would have dismissed such a gift. But she also knew this for what it was—a please-stay gift.

"Now you're a true Alaskan!" Jessie announced, circulating with a tray of mimosas. The declaration hit Sadie unexpectedly—when was the last time anyone had wanted her to belong somewhere just for herself, not for what she could do for them?

Lucky grabbed the microphone, his grin infectious. "A toast to the couple we knew should be a couple even before the couple knew they were a couple! To Kreston and Sadie—proof that sometimes you have to get lost to find your way home."

Sadie caught Kreston watching her, his expression soft. In that moment, surrounded by this collection of bizarre yet wonderful people, she realized her Seattle life had been about managing perceptions, but here it was about being yourself. She'd forgotten how to be herself until Polar Creek.

The jukebox sprang to life with Christmas classics, and Jessie reduced the volume so people could enjoy conversation.

Jessie and Kreston found two empty seats at a table with Lucky, Tucker, and Ten Second Tess, who scooted her chair close to Sadie. "I like you. What's your name?"

She patiently answered. "Sadie."

"Did you know Mayor Collins likes you?" she chirped innocently, as if asking for the first time.

"I heard that, yes," said Sadie, between mouthfuls. The food was so good she wanted to inhale all of it.

Jessie paused her hustle and bustle to join them. "How was your flight this time? Hopefully, not the same as your first wild ride into Polar Creek."

Sadie sipped her mimosa, loving the orange juice and sparkling champagne. "It was magnificent! Oh my God, Jessie, Kreston flew us right next to Denali, and I got to see it up close. We were eye to eye with the summit!" she gushed.

"That's all I could think of for a Christmas gift," said Kreston.

"All you could think of? It's the best one I've ever had." Sadie winked at him. "Well, maybe not the *best* one..." she trailed off, squeezing his hand.

Lucky laughed. "Few get to see Denali up close and personal. Especially on a clear day. However, there's another storm headed our way tomorrow. Another big one from the Bering Sea."

Sadie gave him a coy smile. "This time, I won't mind being stranded."

"How long are you staying?" asked Jessie.

"Until New Year's," replied Sadie. She knew what was coming and braced herself.

"And then what?"

Sadie let it hang there as all eyes at the table darted to her. She sensed Kreston stiffen next to her.

"I'm taking it one day at a time." She said it firmly so no one would press further.

Lucky downed his mimosa. "What are your plans for today, you two?"

Kreston shrugged. "Depends on what Sadie wants to do."

"A Christmas sled dog ride sounds fun." She sent a hopeful glance to Kreston.

"There's your answer," said Lucky, laughing.

Sadie couldn't wait for them to be alone again. She'd become addicted to Polar Creek's charming, irresistible mayor. She rose from the table, put on her jacket, and picked up the box with her bunny boots.

"Come on, Mayor Collins. We have dogs to hook up." She waggled her brows.

He stood up so fast his chair tipped over. "Then we better get going."

Sadie suppressed a laugh at Kreston's unbridled enthusiasm, her insides spinning cartwheels.

"Load up with some of this food," ordered Jessie, motioning to the tables.

"Thanks, Jessie." Sadie hustled over to load two paper plates for their Christmas dinner later on.

Kreston found a cardboard box, and Sadie lowered the plates in, setting napkins over the food. "Merry Christmas, everyone!" they called out, then hurried from the restaurant.

Once they reached his pickup, Kreston opened the truck and set the box of food inside. He gathered Sadie into his arms and planted a kiss on her that would melt an Alaskan volcano.

Sadie's heart lifted to the heavens as she lost herself in him. He topped off the passionate kiss with several light ones. She had the sensation of being watched and swiveled her head toward the restaurant.

There, in the window, were so many faces she couldn't count them all, eagerly watching. She burst out laughing and stepped back from Kreston, who shook his head. "If they want a show, let's give them one. Watch this."

He grabbed her around the waist, leaned her back in a swoon, and kissed her thoroughly, holding the pose until the cheering erupted. Above the commotion, Lucky's distinctive whoops and hollers broke out as Kreston lifted Sadie into the pickup and they sped off.

This was definitely a first for Sadie. And hopefully, it wouldn't be the last.

# Chapter 27

K*reston*
On the way to his place, Kreston remarked, "Jessie said you were good for me."

"Really? In what way?"

"She said you grounded me and added balance to my life." His heart did the tumble thing again, grateful he'd persuaded Sadie to come back. He didn't want to be pushy about her decision to stay beyond another week, but it killed him to be patient.

Kreston thought about the past Christmases he'd spent in Polar Creek. While he'd loved them all, he'd always been the responsible one, the capable one, the one everyone counted on to keep things moving and organize the town's celebrations and activities. He'd filled his empty void by burdening himself with responsibility.

But now, with Sadie here, he was rethinking all of it. To him, it seemed everything he'd done so far in his life had led to the exact moment he'd met Sadie in her impractical boots and ruined suede jacket. Life was full of surprises.

"What are you thinking about?" she asked, studying him.

He glanced at her. "You really want to know, or are you just making conversation?"

"I really want to know."

"Still have those fashionable thigh boots of yours?"

She narrowed her eyes with suspicion. "I've only been dragging them around with me everywhere I've been since they're not functional up here. Why?"

"Functional is a matter of opinion." He gave her a searing look. "For my Christmas present, I want you to put those boots on wearing nothing else...unless you have a G-string and some pasties."

Her eyes widened. "That is honest-to-God what you were thinking?"

"I'm a guy. What'd you expect?" He gave her a lopsided grin.

She laughed. "Or...I could do the same wearing my bunny boots."

Kreston wrinkled his face. "Nah, although you would look hot no matter what boots you put on. But the ones with those tall heels..." He invoked his best California valley accent. "That would *totally* do it for me."

Sadie threw back her head and laughed. "Well, my name isn't Cinnamon, and I'm not an exotic dancer. But I suppose I could arrange something, but minus the pasties." She gave him a coy look. "Maybe after the sled dog ride?"

He perked up. "I can live with those terms."

Behind them in the distance, the town's Christmas lights twinkled, and his sled dogs howled and barked an enthusiastic welcome as he pulled into the driveway. Good friend that he was, Lucky had fed the dogs and plowed his driveway. As he unbuckled and got out, Kreston made a mental note to do something nice for him.

"I can't wait to pet Denali," gushed Sadie. She dove out of her passenger seat and beelined toward the dog lot. "Hi puppy dogs!"

Kreston couldn't help smiling at her delight as they approached the dog yard. The team's excited yips filled the crisp air, their breath creating puffs of vapor in the fading afternoon light. The howling and barking became frenzied as Sadie and Kreston worked their way along the dog line, petting each one as they stood wagging on top of their doghouses.

Kreston grabbed seven harnesses. "Ready for Mushing 101? First rule: never let go of the sled. Second rule: dogs must always be under the musher's control. No exceptions. You can't do one without the other."

He showed her how to harness each dog, explaining their positions and personalities. "Denali's the smartest, and that's why he's the lead dog. He takes after his namesake, proud and strong."

"Like his musher," Sadie teased.

He grinned. "Flattery will get you everywhere. Okay, let's hook them up."

After connecting the dogs to the gangline, Kreston gave her a quick lesson. "Commands are simple: 'Haw' for left. 'Gee' for right. 'Hike' means go and 'whoa' means stop. Got it?"

"So, it's like voicing commands to a Tesla, only with fur and better listening skills?"

Kreston chortled. "Just don't let go of the sled, or you'll be sitting in the snow while your team ends up five miles ahead of you."

"I'm so sorry those snowmachines crashed into your team," said Sadie. "I can't imagine how awful that was."

He nodded grimly. "It was. I hated losing those huskies."

Sadie stroked Denali's fur, letting him snuggle into her. "That would destroy anyone."

"Watch what I do, and you'll get the hang of it." Kreston stepped to the back of the sled to stand on the runners. He demonstrated the commands by mushing the dog team along the road toward Grayling Lake. The Alaskan huskies bounded in perfect synchronization, their excitement a joy to witness.

When they reached Grayling Lake Campground, Kreston halted the team to give Sadie control. She commanded the team like an old pro, mushing the dogs onto the frozen lake through the deep snow, passing the group of empty ice fishing shacks.

"No one's fishing. We have the lake to ourselves," she called out as he hunkered on the sled. The memory of her catching the fish and winning the bet made Kreston smile.

"If Hardware Bob were in town, he and Janet would be out here today. They're ice fishing fanatics." He hoped Bob was improving. It was too bad he and Janet were stuck at the hospital for Christmas.

"Whoa, huskies!" hollered Sadie, and the team halted. "Look, they stopped!" she shouted incredulously.

Kreston laughed, climbing out of the sled. "Of course they did. Hey, check out the sunset." He gazed at the lava-streaked sky and the purple mountains. "Tucker should be out here painting this."

As he set up a portable heater to melt snow for dog water, he noted Sadie taking in this Alaskan vibe—vapor clouds from panting dogs, the untouched snowy landscape, and the moon beginning to rise as the sun dipped below the mountains.

"Kreston, thank you for all of this. I love this so much!" Arms outstretched, Sadie spun in a joyful circle, her exuberance warming him. A long-buried flame flickered to life inside his chest.

Sadie was a natural musher. He was impressed by her confident commands and how she handled his dog team.

He bit his tongue before saying, "Enough to move here and stay with me?" He didn't want to pressure her or rush her decision.

Kreston took control of the sled, wearing a headlamp to light his way as he mushed his team home. When they reached his place, Sadie helped him water and feed the dogs. He was impressed she'd memorized each dog's name and could point out their individual personalities.

When they finished, they hurried inside. Kreston built a fire while Sadie heated Jessie's Christmas feast in his well-equipped kitchen. The log home soon filled with warmth and delicious aromas, but Kreston was interested more in Sadie than the food. She moved through his space easily, like she belonged there, humming Christmas carols as she worked. He refused to dwell on the fact she may not be staying after New Year's. He hoped for the best, but so far, she hadn't given him any sign one way or the other.

After dinner, they settled in front of the fire with hot buttered rums.

Sadie abruptly rose. "Back in a minute. Got things to do." She left the room.

Kreston rested his head back and closed his eyes, letting the whirlwind of the past several days settle in his brain. Deciding to fly to Talkeetna from Anchorage had turned out to be one of his better decisions. Sadie wouldn't be here if he hadn't done it.

He gave himself a pat on the back for that one, crossing his fingers for a positive outcome.

# Chapter 28

K*reston*

Kreston's eyes opened upon hearing the opening strains of Eartha Kitt's "Santa Baby." Sadie stood squarely in front of him, holding her singing fish trophy and swaying to the beat.

What she wore hypnotized him, and Little Kreston sat up and took notice.

The way she filled out the red bra had his undivided attention. His eyes drifted down to the matching lacy red thong, then down to those thigh-high boots he'd jokingly hinted she should wear.

Sadie sang along with "Santa Baby," wiggling her shoulders back and forth in a cutesy style of dance, like Betty Boop in the old cartoons, her copper hair draped over her shoulders.

His breaths caught so much he thought he might choke. Her playful performance had him collapsing with laughter at the end. But when she set the fish plaque down and straddled his lap, the laughter faded into sudden awareness of Little Kreston pushing up against her.

He swallowed. "Nice performance," he choked out, his voice raspy.

"Thank you, Mayor Collins." Her eyes widened, and he could tell she felt Little Kreston rising to the occasion. She leaned forward and kissed him lightly. "Merry Christmas. I haven't had time to get you anything, so this will have to do."

He smoothed his palm down her back, loving the feel of her soft skin. "You coming back with me is my Christmas present." He was aware of the huskiness in his voice. All he knew was he wanted her.

She glanced at the large bear rug splayed on the floor in front of the fire. "Make love to me on the bear rug." Her seductive smile was enough to undo him.

Right now, if she asked him to go outside and make love in the snow, he would. He'd do anything she asked. He lifted her from his lap, and she stood. But before he could rise from his chair, Sadie plunked her foot onto his thigh.

"Will you help me unzip?" She licked her lips with a comical wink.

"Do Seattle women catch the biggest fish?" He gazed up at her as his brain indicator slid to empty. He couldn't believe this was happening.

*Am I dreaming?*

His eyes traveled up her leg to the rest of her, towering over him, one-hundred-fifty percent female. He locked gazes with her as he moved his hand up her leg to her thigh, where his fingers found the zipper. It took every ounce of restraint to lower his hand ever so slowly, unzipping her boot to the ankle and exposing the pale skin of her calf.

Sadie lowered her foot and tugged off the boot. She raised her other foot and rested it on his thigh so he could do the same. This time, he unzipped it quickly, and she tugged it off and tossed it behind her.

Kreston stood and lifted his long-sleeved t-shirt over his head and dropped it. Then he removed the rest of his clothes. He took Sadie's hand and pulled her down to the bear rug with him.

The fire's warmth was nothing compared to the heat speeding through his veins.

"Do you Alaskan guys fantasize about having women on bear rugs next to fires?" she purred.

"Well, yeah, it's always been one of my fantasies," he breathed, kissing her neck as she lay beside him. "Women think we're more complicated than we really are."

She offered him a cat-eyed look. "You know you're a cliché, right?"

"And proud of it." He moved his hand under one bra strap and stretched it off her shoulder.

The black, silky fur and the sparkle of the fire heightened his awareness of her. He kissed her slow, soft, and sensual. She sat up and reached around to unclasp her sexy little bra.

"I love this on you, but it looks better off." He helped her out of it, causing his heart to skitter and increasing the ache in Little Kreston.

He kissed her smooth skin, roaming his hands over her. His fingertips found the front of her thong. He eased it down and off her legs, tossing it.

She tugged him down on top of her, breathless. "I want you inside me, Mayor Collins."

He'd planned more foreplay because he was procedural and a linear kind of guy. But if she wanted him inside her pearly gates, he was happy to park himself inside of them.

He reached down low and massaged her center, surprised to find she was more than ready for him. He tore open a packet with his teeth, dressed Little Kreston, and moved on top of her. She yielded to him, feeling soft as velvet. He joined their bodies, moving slowly at first, then speeding up his rhythm.

When she arched, stiffened, and cried out her release, he felt her pulsating around Little Kreston. God, he loved the female body—loved pleasuring her this way. He soon joined her in his own euphoric release, then settled beside her with a contented sigh.

They intertwined like pretzels while she rubbed his muscled back. Her gentle touch had catapulted his libido to the stratosphere so many times he'd lost count. She wrapped herself around him like a soft blanket.

"We fit together like two puzzle pieces," she whispered, her eyes catching the fire's reflection.

He lost himself in them, brushing back her hair. "We just made a Christmas memory."

"Yes, we did. You look sexy with that scruffy face." She ran the back of her hand over his cheeks and chin.

"I had a beard when I first moved here, wanting to fit in. Got rid of it when mosquitoes landed in it."

Sadie burst out laughing. "Would have loved to see that."

This is what he'd missed. The sex, sure, but it was the shared intimacy with her that truly made him happy. Last night, she'd whispered how cherished he made her feel. If he had his way, that feeling would only grow stronger with time.

He yawned, causing Sadie to yawn. "I'll snuff this fire, then let's go to bed."

"I'm up for that." She stood and bent to pick up the clothes they'd tossed.

"You're beautiful in the firelight, Sadie. I could lie here forever looking at you."

She extended her hand to help him to his feet. "Ditto, Mayor Collins."

When they crawled into bed, Kreston knew with absolute certainty that this was more than attraction, more than affection. Every moment felt precious, sacred, meant to be remembered...no matter how this turned out.

"What are you thinking?" she murmured against his chest as he wrapped his arms around her.

"I've never had a Christmas like this." He pressed a kiss to her copper hair. "Usually, I'm checking the generator at the hotel or seeing to frozen pipes."

"I think Polar Creek can do without you for tonight." She snuggled into him. "Maybe it's time you trust others to handle things now and then?"

"I'm used to being Johnny on the spot for everyone. If you weren't here, it's what I'd be doing."

"And working yourself to death. You, my friend, must learn how to delegate. Didn't they teach you delegation at that expensive East Coast business school?"

"Yes, but when I got to Alaska, I felt like I had to be all things to all people because of my past failures."

She traced his jaw with her fingertip. "You know, watching you with the dogs today... I realized you aren't just the capable mayor who fixes everything. You're an amazing blend of strength and tenderness. The way you care for everything—the dogs, the town, and me..."

His heart swelled. "Sadie, please say you'll stay. Not just until New Year's. Stay for good."

The way she looked at him, he could tell something was bothering her. "I promise I'll think about it, but...do you realize what I would be giving up? A lifetime of building a career..." she trailed off, shaking her head.

"I gave up the same thing," he said quietly. "Granted, not by choice, but in the long run, it turned out to be the best path for me. It's okay not to be a hundred percent sure of our decisions. Sometimes it's good to take a risk—close your eyes and take the leap."

"Let's talk about this later, okay? Right now, I want our perfect Christmas to stay perfect." She closed her eyes, and he studied her as she drifted off.

He chided himself for pressuring her. He hadn't meant to but couldn't help himself.

Moonbeams came through his bedroom window, bathing Sadie's face in a silvery glow.

That's when it hit him—the best Christmas gifts were never the ones you planned for. They were the surprises that crashed into your life when you least expected them. Like a woman in thigh-high boots with a killer smile, singing "Santa Baby" while brandishing a mechanical fish.

He drew Sadie closer, breathing in the sweet scent of her hair and marveling at the twist of fate that had brought her into his life.

Best. Christmas. Ever.

# Chapter 29

S*adie. New Year's Eve*

On New Year's Eve morning, Sadie snuggled closer to Kreston, breathing in his familiar scent of pine and wood smoke. The days since Christmas had slipped away like water through her fingers. Between organizing Kreston's office and computer files, and helping Jessie handle the restaurant rushes, she'd lost all track of time.

She treasured these lazy mornings with Kreston, their easy routine feeling more natural each day. Yet beneath it lurked an impossible choice and she remained paralyzed with indecision: cling to the familiar or leap into the unknown? A week had passed, and she was no closer to her answer.

Sensing he was awake, Sadie rolled over to look Kreston in the eye. "You know what I realized? Everything in my life has centered on appearances. But here, it's not like that."

Kreston's arms tightened around her. "That's what happens when you spend time in Alaska. Pretense is stripped away. You can't fake your way through a blizzard." He propped himself on his elbow. "What more can I do to convince you to stay?"

She avoided his question by reaching for his morning erection and stroking him. "This."

"Oh, God," he moaned. "Keep doing that, and I'll never leave this bed. Unfortunately, I'd better get to town and help set up for tonight's New Year's Eve party. You can stay here and sleep if you like."

"Are you kidding? And miss the chaos?" She laughed. "Not on your life."

"I'll make the coffee." He flung back his comforter and stood, stretching, with his back to her.

Sadie admired the view. How could she leave this? Leave him? She still had to sort everything out. It was easy to procrastinate her decision while spending time with Kreston and helping with his daily tasks.

After feeding the dogs—who now greeted her like family—she and Kreston gathered their party clothes to take into town with them. Sadie grabbed her sparkly cocktail dress from the bottom of her suitcase, and they climbed into the truck and headed to town.

The Community Center hummed with pre-party energy. Hardware Bob was back, looking remarkably well after his heart scare. He supervised the installation of the massive disco ball while Janet fussed over the sound system. Sadie found herself swept into the preparations, moving between helping Jessie in the hotel kitchen and arranging tables with Aloha in the party room. Aloha announced each centerpiece placement like it was breaking news.

"Aloha, Mayor Kreston and Mayor Kreston's girlfriend!" she greeted them. "You two look chipper today." She had her usual deck of cards in her hands, shuffling away.

As Sadie hurried from the Crooked Spoon with a snack tray, Ten Second Tess appeared in the lobby, clutching something glittery. "I made these for you since you're Mayor Collins' girlfriend. What's your name?"

"Sadie." She extended her palm.

"I made you a present, Sadie." Tess offered her a pair of sequined earrings and a matching headband.

"Thank you, Tess." The handmade gift brought tears to Sadie's eyes. She immediately put on the earrings and stretched the headband around her head, pulling her hair over it.

"Now I look more like 1970s disco. What do you think?" She turned her head side-to-side to show off the earrings.

"They look nice. You know, Kreston likes you." Tess dashed off and disappeared up the stairs.

While Sadie arranged food platters with Jessie, Hardware Bob and Janet cornered her.

"You know," Janet said thoughtfully, "hardly anyone we met in Anchorage had heard of Polar Creek."

"Criminal, really," Bob added. "All this beauty, these stories, these people... someone should tell the world about us. Not to attract people to move here, but to increase our tourism. We need a share of the Alaskan tourism dollars. Then we could build a post office and move it out of the hotel. We could even hire a postal employee."

"Not that Kreston does a terrible job or anything," Janet emphasized. "It's just he's burdened with so much."

"I've been lecturing him to delegate more." A thought exploded inside Sadie's brain. "I have an idea. We should create a tourism office. Set up a website, advertise to the world Polar Creek is an exciting tourist destination. We just need to get the word out."

*Why hadn't I thought of this before?*

Janet thought for a moment. "You said 'we.' Does that mean you're staying? Everyone's been saying you'll be gone after tomorrow."

Reality hit Sadie like a grenade. "I—I guess I could stay a little longer to help set one up—if Kreston thinks it's a good idea. Everyone would have to vote on it..." Her mind raced with newfound possibilities.

Janet smiled. "You should consider it. We'd love for you to stay. You would be a wonderful asset to this town."

Her words warmed Sadie. Before she decided anything, she'd talk with Kreston. But now wasn't the time with the frenzied preparations for tonight's New Year's soiree.

Sadie crossed Main Street to the hotel. She stood for a moment on the sidewalk, soaking in the familiar rhythms and heartbeat of Polar Creek; people were busy doing errands and making their usual social rounds. Life was predictable here, and she liked that. She opened the hotel door and walked inside. Out of habit, she headed upstairs as if going to her old hotel room.

Since returning to Polar Creek, she'd stayed with Kreston. But she'd missed the hustle and bustle of this hotel. And she missed Aloha, Ten Second Tess, and Jessie humming around the hotel, doing their part to keep things running. Sadie turned in time to catch Tess closing the door of the ice maker and sprinting down the stairs.

Curious, Sadie moved to the ice maker and opened the door. A pile of Christmas decorations mixed with tiny shampoos rested on the ice chunks. She smiled and left everything where it was, knowing that organizing things in her own way gave Tess purpose. What had happened to Tess still tugged at Sadie's heart, but the girl seemed happy, and that was the important thing.

It was nearing the time for the party, and Sadie realized she didn't have a place to change. She tapped down the stairs and headed for Kreston's office. It was empty, so she dressed in her party finery, applied makeup, and adjusted Tess's glittery headband in her hair. She hesitated before slipping her feet into the stilettos. Nope. The Alaskan way was to wear your boots outside and carry your heels to wear inside. It had already become a habit.

Carrying her stilettoes, Sadie stepped out of the hotel to see others heading to the Community Center. Some were on foot, and others had arrived in their snowmachines, trucks, and SUVs. Strains of "Disco Inferno" met her ears as she swung open one of the front double doors.

She wondered if Kreston had taken time to change into his tux. She loved seeing him in it and couldn't wait. She also couldn't wait to tell him about her tourism office idea. Once inside, she walked around but didn't see him. He must have gotten hung up with something. Or someone.

Jessie ran up to her. "Have you seen Aloha?"

Sadie shook her head. "No, I just came over from the hotel and didn't see her. Figured she was here. Why?"

"Someone saw her running down Main Street, crying. She seemed upset," explained Jessie. "She must have run home. She only lives three blocks away."

"What's the house number?" asked Sadie. "I'll go see what's going on."

Jessie relayed the address as Sadie changed into her boots and bundled up. "Be back soon. Keep things going until Kreston returns, okay?"

Sadie stepped out, then briskly walked down Main Street and turned right onto Spruce Street. She spotted the tiny pink house Jessie had described. She hurried up the steps and knocked.

To her surprise, Kreston answered.

"What's going on? Is Aloha okay?"

He looked relieved. "Glad you're here. Come on in."

Sadie walked into the small living room to see Aloha sitting on her couch, hugging a pillow. She rocked back and forth, tears streaming down her cheeks. She lifted her face and smiled.

"I remember!" she said to Sadie. "I got my memory back! I remember everything! I have a house on a beach in Honolulu. And it's a big one!"

Sadie noted she didn't say 'aloha' first.

"Seriously?" Sadie sat next to her, stunned. "How did this happen?"

"I'll explain." Kreston settled into a chair across from the two women. "I was walking into the hotel this afternoon, and Aloha bumped into me as she ran out, crying. I ran after her and followed her here. Turns out, she'd fallen and hit her head. Now she remembers what happened before Costco."

Sadie rested her hand on Aloha's knee. "What do you remember?"

"I was... am... a professional poker player. One of the best in Hawaii." Aloha laughed. "I made millions reading other player's tells, remembering every card played. Had a reputation as 'The Aloha Shark' because I'd yell 'Aloha' before taking their money."

Sadie's mouth hung open. "A poker player? Like the ones on TV?" She exchanged incredulous looks with Kreston.

Aloha nodded. "I flew to Anchorage for a secret high-stakes game. Someone found out I was counting cards and whipped out a handgun. He chased me, and I ran out into the snow. I slipped on the ice, hit my head…" She touched the spot where she'd bumped it again today. "Next thing I knew, I was rounding up shopping carts and welcoming everyone to Costco."

Sadie glanced at Kreston, then back to Aloha. "This is a wild story. Are you sure this isn't just a dream?"

"No, watch this!" Aloha picked up her deck of cards from the coffee table and dealt them each a hand of poker, her hands flying so fast Sadie couldn't keep track.

"Aloha! That's why you're always shuffling cards. You didn't forget that part of you. This is incredible!" She gazed at Aloha in awe.

"Look, I haven't lost my knack." Aloha scooped up the cards and showed them a couple of fast moves, then spread the deck out with a flourish, better than any Vegas casino dealer.

"Couldn't tell you how I wound up in the Costco parking lot, though. A shopper must have given me a ride and dropped me off there. Then I ran into Kreston, and he helped me," she said happily.

"Wow, a professional poker player?" Sadie said, astonished. "Never would have guessed."

"Me either," Aloha and Kreston chorused, and everyone laughed.

"How are you feeling? Do you want Janet to examine your head?" asked Kreston.

Aloha rubbed it. "I'm sure it's okay. Not bleeding or anything." She looked up at him. "Thank you for coming to make sure I was all right."

"That's what friends are for," he responded.

"So, what are you going to do now?" Sadie asked Aloha, who suddenly perked up.

"Money! I have money! Lots of it. I have to check my bank accounts." She got up and paced back and forth. "I'm a millionaire several times over. I invested the money I won, and it must be worth a heck of a lot after five years."

"Wouldn't someone have declared you missing or dead and taken your money by now?" asked Sadie.

Aloha shook her head. "I don't have heirs, and my parents are deceased. Hey, you two, want to take a trip to Hawaii next week? I have business to take care of. I'll pay your way." She grinned at Kreston. "Maybe after, I can pay for those streetlamps you've been wanting to put on Main Street."

He gave her a look of surprise. "You don't have to do that."

"Yes, I do! I'm grateful for what you've done for me. It's the least I can do for you," gushed Aloha.

Sadie laughed. "I would love to go to Hawaii!" Then she remembered and shook her head. "Except I don't know what I'm doing next week."

Kreston's eyes flicked to hers, but to his credit, he said nothing.

Aloha wiped her eyes. "The funny thing is, I love who I became here, in Polar Creek. The real me was sick and tired of the poker scene. Here, I learned to love people instead of reading them for a poker hand."

"So, you're choosing Polar Creek over Hawaii?" Sadie asked in disbelief.

"Yep. I need to take care of my old life in Honolulu, and transfer my bank accounts to Alaska, and then, maybe I'll start a poker night at the Crooked Spoon." Aloha gave Kreston a mischievous look.

"Uh, we'll discuss that minor detail later," he said uneasily, shifting in his chair. He glanced up at a wall clock. "We have a party to go to."

Sadie hugged Aloha. "I'm so happy your memory returned. What a gift that is." As they put on their winter garb and headed out the door, Sadie took Kreston's arm and squeezed it. "I love that you checked on her."

"I'm just happy you can remember now," he said to Aloha.

"Me too!" She jumped around like a pogo stick. "Wait'll everyone hears about this!" Aloha wriggled into her coat and dashed out the door to tell everyone her big news.

# Chapter 30

S*adie*

As Sadie and Kreston headed inside to the New Year's Eve party at the Community Center, loud voices and laughing greeted them. It was only an hour until midnight. Kreston took Sadie's coat and hung it up in the foyer outside of the main room.

"You look stunning, as always." He tugged Sadie into him. "Thanks for showing up at Aloha's. I was worried when she ran off the way she did. Thank God it wasn't anything horrific."

"You feel responsible for her since you're the one who found her with her amnesia, don't you?" Sadie gazed up at him with admiration.

He nodded. "Couldn't just leave her there. God knows what would have happened to her. I didn't want her to wind up living in a cardboard box on Northern Lights Boulevard in Anchorage, freezing to death."

Sadie hugged him. "I've not met anyone like you." She smiled at a couple coming through the door, then turned to Kreston. "Can we talk for a minute? I have something to say before we roll into the next year."

"Talk fast. There's only an hour left." He led her to his office and unlocked the door. Once they were inside, he locked it. "Don't want interruption."

Sadie arranged herself in one chair in front of his desk. She motioned to the other. "Have a seat, Mayor Collins. Let's take a meeting. I have some official business to propose."

He sat, waiting expectantly. "Go on."

"This town needs a tourism office," she began. "Real marketing, not tourist-trap stuff. Alaska Magazine ads, a website, the whole nine yards."

He gave her a blank look. "Uh, huh."

"Hardware Bob and his wife Janet told me the people they met in Anchorage weren't familiar with Polar Creek. No one had even heard of it, much less knew where it was. That gave me an idea. I think I could earn your town coffers some cash. Bob suggested maybe you could afford to build a post office."

Kreston sat back in the chair and folded his arms. "What's your point?"

"My point is...my point is..." she struggled for the words. Why was this so flipping hard?

He waited with another blank look.

"You'd need someone to run it, and—"

He cut her off. "Does this mean you're staying?" His voice was neutral, but his eyes held galaxies of hope.

She lifted her gaze to his, and her eyes watered. "Yes," she said, her voice barely audible. She cleared her throat. "I mean YES! Yes! Yes! I'm staying!" She flew out of her chair and threw herself at him.

He caught her and hugged her so hard her insides squeezed. "Good. Because there's this one little detail I have to tell you...I love you."

Tears spilled out as she buried her face in the side of his neck. "I've loved you from the moment I was born. I just didn't know it until you opened that stupid door to Lucky's plane."

"I promise not to pressure you about anything else." Kreston wiped her tears with his thumbs. "I know you like to take things one day at a time."

"You know me well, don't you?"

"Beginning to," he said. "Each new thing I discover makes me love you more. Like how you patiently tell Ten Second Tess your name whenever she asks. How you laugh at Lucky's jokes even if they aren't funny. And the way you check on people and help them, same as I do. We're two peas in a pod, Sadie-kins. And I love you for it."

She got up from his lap, scooted her chair close, and sat in it. She took his hands in hers. "Come with me to Seattle to help me pack up my stuff. I have quite the swanky digs, so I'll have to sell most of it. But here's the thing: I don't want to lose you, and I know you'll never leave Polar Creek. I'm willing to move up here to Alaska so we can be together."

"You don't know how this makes me feel—" he started.

Sadie raised a finger. "But—I must earn my way. I still want to continue public relations work. So, on that note...will you hire me to be Polar Creek's public relations person for your new tourism office?"

He thought for a minute, and she could tell his wheels were going ninety in that overloaded brain of his. A smile took shape and widened into a grin. "Maybe if what Aloha says is true, she'll loan us the money to start it."

"I know where I can get an expensive diamond engagement ring to sell." She winked. "I also have a sizeable chunk squirreled away in investments."

"Now that, I can help you with." Kreston's brows rose. "Selling that ring would be worth a flight to Anchorage."

"Oh, and while we're there, let's look into getting that GPS tracker device for Ten Second Tess."

Kreston paused. "This is one reason I love you. Always thinking of everyone else."

Sadie confessed, "When Aloha said she'd rather stay in Polar Creek than return to Hawaii, it kicked my decision over into the 'yes' column."

Kreston rose and grasped her hands to lift her to her feet. He moved in for a kiss when he heard distant whoops and hollers.

"Wait, we're missing the party!" Kreston unlocked the door and flung it open.

"I want to be under the disco ball with you at midnight." Sadie took his arm and steered out the door toward the Community Center.

They walked in to see everyone dancing the disco era dance, The Bump, to "That's The Way I Like It" by KC & The Sunshine Band. Kreston looked at his phone. "Ten minutes, baby. Dance with me." He swung her onto the dance floor, and they bumped with the best of them.

Ten Second Tess boogied over and gave Kreston a hip bump, then did it to Sadie. She moved off, and Lucky twirled over, doing his up-and-down disco point like John Travolta in *Saturday Night Fever.*

Hardware Bob had rigged the twirling silver disco ball to fill the room with specks of light, giving off the illusion that everyone danced like professionals no matter how much they sucked at it.

As midnight approached, Kreston took up his traditional position with the microphone on the stage with the town musicians. Watching him, Sadie admired the impossibly handsome mayor who ran everything, fixed everything...a man who'd built this community, one act of generosity at a time.

Kreston began the countdown. "Ten! Nine! Eight!"

The countdown felt like more than a year ticking away—it was Sadie's old life falling away, making room for a brand new one. One she never in a million years would have imagined for herself.

"Seven! Six! Five!"

Kreston looked so hot up there—despite his not having time to change into his tuxedo—and it was all she could do not to run up and jump his bones right on the spot.

"Four! Three! Two! One! HAPPY NEW YEAR!" Kreston threw his arms in the air, handed off the mic, and jumped down from the stage platform. He beelined straight for Sadie, who held out her arms to receive him.

Kreston's kiss tasted like the promise of wonderful things to come. "Happy New Year, Polar Creek chick." He grinned, and she knew this was right. She could tell her decision had made him happy, and he didn't care who knew it. It made her happy, too.

When they broke apart, he grabbed Sadie's hand and pulled her up onto the platform. He picked up the microphone, his eyes never leaving hers.

"I have an announcement," he said into the mic. "Polar Creek is growing. We've just gained a new permanent resident. And we're establishing a tourism office. I'd like to present the new director of the Polar Creek Tourism Office—Sadie Foster!"

The celebration that erupted was mind-numbing, yet heartwarming.

"When's the wedding?" Tall Martha called out.

"Mayor Collins has a girlfriend? What's her name?" yelled Ten Second Tess.

"Congratulations and *Slàinte*!" Tucker hollered, holding up a shot of Jameson. "May your marketing be as vast as Alaska's wilderness, and your website gets hits like mosquito swarms in June!"

Everyone tittered, and more music played.

"Aloha! You two can go to Hawaii with me!" Aloha cried out, clapping.

Jessie rushed up and hugged Sadie with such force it knocked the breath from her lungs. She clutched her like a mother who'd just learned her child was coming home. She pulled back and cradled Sadie's face with watery eyes.

"I knew you'd choose the best path. I just knew it!" Jessie's voice cracked. "Family doesn't always have to be blood. You have a new family now."

A warmth spread through Sadie's chest, filling all the empty spaces.

Everyone seemed genuinely happy. Suddenly, the opening chords of "We Are Family" burst from the speakers, and the room erupted. Lucky grabbed Bob, Tucker seized Janet, and suddenly a wild Conga line snaked between tables.

Kreston's hands found Sadie's waist, spinning her into the chain of laughing, stumbling dancers. His deep voice rumbled against her ear, delightfully off-key, and Sadie dissolved into the moment of sheer joy...of belonging somewhere at last.

"I'll bake welcome muffins," volunteered Jessie. "Every morning until you're sick of them."

"We're going to Hawaii!" bellowed Aloha, who'd informed everyone her real name was Nalani Lua. "It'll take getting used to, but I'll still answer to Aloha, don't worry. Did you know I'm rich?" she repeated to anyone who would listen.

Ten Second Tess embraced Sadie. "Mayor Collins loves you, so I love you. What is your name?"

Sadie hugged her tight, tears flowing freely at her sincere sentiment. "My name is Sadie. And I love you, too."

Looking around at these beautiful, crazy people—her people now—Sadie felt the last piece of her heart click into place. Bob and Janet were already discussing website designs. Lucky was composing tourism slogans, and Tucker was busy sketching a logo. The Gossip Trio was discussing her welcome party because this town looked for any excuse to have a party. It broke the winter monotony, warded off cabin fever, and gave everyone something to look forward to.

Sadie figured the best new beginnings must come disguised as diverted flights and broken plans. Her true home had tapped her on the shoulder when she wasn't looking. Who knew it would be a tiny Alaskan town where the weather report is always shitty to partly shitty...where the mayor organizes mail by street but can't match his socks, and those who forget your name love you exactly as you are.

It was clear to Sadie that her path had pointed to Kreston from the beginning; she'd just been too blindsided by hurt and rejection to realize it. Everyone else saw it long before she did.

As Kreston pulled her close for another kiss, Sadie knew this wasn't just another new year. This was a new life. And a second chance with a new love. One with staying power.

Her heart now belonged to the hottest mayor in Alaska. "I love you, Mayor Collins."

"Right back atcha," he breathed in her ear, kissing it. "Happy New Year, Miss Tourism Director."

"I'll wear my 'Santa Baby' outfit for you when we get home," she purred.

"I can't wait. Just got to get everything secured here first." He stole a quick kiss. "On second thought, I think I'll let someone else handle it." Kreston took her hand and led her to the door. "Let's go home."

Home.

Sadie liked the sound of that. She dashed out the door, not bothering to change into her bunny boots, with Kreston on her heels.

*T*hanks so much for reading! If you enjoyed it, please tell your friends and family about it and I'd appreciate you posting a review on Amazon. Reviews make a big difference for my success as a writer. Scroll to the end for my Polar Creek Christmas recipes!

*If you enjoyed this story, check out my other romantic comedies. Download Cupid's Kerfuffle[1], a free romcom in the Polar Paired Romance Comedy Series by signing up for my VIP Readers List!*
*Hello Spain, Goodbye Heart*
*Irish Thunder*
*Cupid's Kefuffle*
*Everybody Loves Polar Bears*

Read on for a taste of *Everybody Loves Polar Bears!*
Chapter 1

"Stop! Don't shoot!" Macy Applegate held her arm out in a stop motion as her pulse raced. The urgency in her words caused every head in the room to swivel in her direction.

"Polar bears deserve to exist the same as humans do. I won't let you shoot them!" Macy poured her heart and soul into every word.

---

1. *https://dl.bookfunnel.com/q9nsmlcw6v*

"Get out of my way, or I'll shoot *you*," growled the man in a menacing tone.

She lifted her chin and studied him. Her mind blanked when she locked onto the glacial stare of the fair-haired man firmly planted in front of her.

"Um... where did I leave off?" She frantically searched for her line, clutching the pages with trembling fingers.

"I'll have to shoot you," he said impatiently, waving his folded script.

"I sure hope not." Macy raised her eyes to find him watching her. She fought to control her nerves and let out an impatient sigh. "May I please start again? I lost my concentration." Heat radiated her cheeks as she chastised herself for her lack of professionalism.

"No," he said tersely. "Continue." He glanced at his wristwatch, then crossed his arms as if he had something better to do.

Nick Westwood had introduced himself as the assistant director for this movie. Before her audition, she'd looked up the production staff online. Westwood had earned a stellar reputation in the film industry—probably why he was so snooty.

He offered her an expectant, disgruntled look. "Well? I'm not getting any younger here."

She sucked in a deep breath so as not to call him a smartass. Instead, she focused on her sides from the script. "Don't want to shoot you," she read, punching each word while she meant the opposite.

"Wrong line. Yours is the one *after* that." His condescension gave her the impression he thought her to be one click short of being an idiot.

Normally, she was calm and composed during an audition, but her nerves jangled whenever she glanced at this guy with his beauty-school-dropout tousled hair. She figured he deliberately styled it to mimic a windswept look, like he'd just blown in from trekking a nearby glacier.

"Sorry. I knew that." Her cheeks heated as she put her finger on the next line, afraid she'd mess it up. "I'm determined to save these polar bears. If I must, I'll take a bullet for them—" She stopped and grimaced.

Westwood's mosaics of blue ice locked her in a stony stare. "Why'd you stop? Keep going." He darted another glance at his wristwatch.

*I must be taking up too much time,* she chided herself.

Macy leaned in to examine the script, and in the name of taking up even more time, she pointed something out. "Hate to toss a monkey wrench into this, but does it really make sense for this character to say she'd take a bullet for a polar bear? It sounds like dialogue from a cheesy 'B' movie. But who am I to judge? I'm not a screenwriter," she added sweetly.

Westwood cocked a brow. "*Everybody Loves Polar Bears* is a movie about saving polar bears from extinction," he said with an air of condescension.

"My understanding is this movie is also about conserving arctic marine life and preventing population declines of keystone species in a climate change environment. Polar bears being one of those keystone species," she said with an air of authority.

"That's what I said in a nutshell." Curiosity wrinkled his face. "And you know this because?"

"I study this subject in my line of work. It's right there on my resume." She pointed.

He glanced down at a clipboard on the small table next to him. "I see, but you aren't here to evaluate the script. Please read what's there. Cripes, everyone's a critic," he muttered, giving her a hard look. "And let's see some emotion this time."

*I'll bet he practices that crabby expression in the mirror to unnerve people. You want emotion? I'll give you some emotion, buddy.*

Resolute, Macy cleared her throat, eyeballing the camera on its tripod, the blinking red light reminding her it was recording. She pictured Westwood aiming an AR-15 on a blinky-eyed polar bear so she'd have motivation to narrow her gaze into a killer stink-eye.

"If you shoot these bears, I guarantee it'll be the *last* thing you ever shoot!" she growled, punching every word. She almost said 'punk' like Harry Callahan in the 1970s *Dirty Harry* movie, but it was a tad outdated.

Westwood flinched and cocked a brow. "That's not what the script says."

"I tweaked it to be more plausible. Don't you think?" Macy beamed at him.

"I believe we're done here. Thanks for coming in," he said in a clipped manner.

Her proud smile dribbled to the floor. "But I'm not finished! Let me start over—I'm a local stage actress—I have excellent reviews with lead roles. Like I said, it's all on my resume—"

He cut in. "I understand, but we've heard enough. Thank you." He nudged the man sitting beside him, tapping maniacally on his phone. "Josh, get her headshot before she goes."

The dark-haired man raised his phone. He smirked, ogling her with a lingering once-over. "Smile, beautiful."

She tried forcing her mouth upward, but all she could summon was a stunned, pissed-off expression. If they needed a disgruntled extra, she could totally play that part. In spades.

The other guy tapped his phone to photograph her, then went back to splitting atoms or whatever the heck else he was doing.

"But... I'd like to finish this scene," she pleaded. "I spent the entire weekend preparing for this audition. I can do this. I'm just nervous."

"Everyone is nervous when they audition." Westwood flashed her a stiff but pearly smile.

Macy was no stranger to auditioning—she knew the sting of obvious rejection but stayed composed out of principle. She regarded Nick Westwood with an unblinking stare. Despite her twisted insides, she steeled herself.

"You didn't like my audition, did you?" she challenged.

Westwood picked up the clipboard with her audition sheet. "You did fine."

"But not good enough, right? Let me do it again. Give me a chance, please..." Begging wasn't her style, but she wanted this badly. She tried to gauge Westwood's expression behind his cool mask of indifference but could only guess what he was thinking, since his glacial stare matched his frosty demeanor.

"Trust me, you did great," he repeated, his voice devoid of expression, as he scribbled on her audition sheet.

*I know where this is heading. Nowhere.*

Macy sized the guy up. Hollywood handsome and then some, a few crow's feet from squinting in the L.A. sunshine. She guessed him to be thirty-five, maybe forty if he did Botox, which he probably did. They all did. The muscular arms and broad shoulders told her he was no stranger to a gym.

"Miss Applegate?"

She snapped out of her jaded assessment. "Yes?"

"We'll be in touch, to let you know."

"Thank you," Macy forced out. The words stuck like toads in her throat. She didn't stand a snowball's chance of getting cast in this movie.

Macy pictured Westwood next to his outdoor pool at his palatial digs up on Mulholland Drive, tall palms waving, the Hollywood Hills framing him while he barked into his phone with a studio executive—his bathrobe strategically hung open so his household staff could swoon over his gym-centric body.

"Thanks for coming in." Westwood's finger brushed hers as she handed him the script pages. She caught the scent of a great-smelling cologne, reeking of Rodeo Drive.

His eyes swept over her like an icy wave, and for a millisecond she thought she detected a smidgeon of amiability. But then, this guy couldn't be friendly if his life depended on it.

"I look forward to hearing from you," she said authoritatively, as if she were the one casting this movie. As she put on her bright-colored Alaskan parka, she noticed Westwood eyeballing it.

"This isn't real fur," she rushed to explain, fingering the arctic fox fur ruff around the hood and cuffs. It was indeed real, but she didn't want the Hollywood contingent regarding Alaskans as animal-trapping savages. Then again, why should she care?

*Because I want a part in this movie.*

Macy berated herself for her last-ditch suck-up effort to get cast.

"I wasn't judging," Westwood tossed out lamely. His baseball cap sported a fighting salmon with a lure in its mouth.

*Aww, how quaint: Hollywood guy wants to fit in with the locals.*

"When can I expect to hear from you?" she asked as she removed her heels and bent to tug on her *Xtratufs* snow boots.

He stood with folded arms, studying her. "Someone will be in touch."

She waited for the when, but he didn't give her one. Instead, his words hung in the air between them like a suspension bridge over a rushing glacial river.

*So much for this audition.*

"Well, thank you. Good luck with your production." Macy picked up her purse from a nearby chair and turned to go.

"Miss Applegate?" Westwood called after her. "What's your reason for auditioning for *Everybody Loves Polar Bears?*"

She twisted around in surprise and stared at him like he'd sprouted fairy wings.

*Isn't it obvious? Is this guy for real?*

"Everyone has a reason. What do you hope to get out of this if we cast you?" He looked at her expectantly.

"All right." She thought for a moment. "Polar bears are at the top of the food chain and play a vital role in the overall health of the Arctic marine environment. This movie will raise awareness of the plight of this species that is heading toward extinction. Without polar bears, the food chain would be severely disrupted..." she trailed off, catching his amused stare.

"You sound like an environmental impact statement." He folded his arms and smirked, as if he'd heard this reasoning countless times. "Now, tell me the real reason."

"That *is* the real reason," she bristled, unappreciative of his deprecating attitude.

What the heck would Mr. Congeniality know about environmental impact statements? That was *her* line of work.

"Everyone wants to save the polar bears. Now, instead of narrating a National Geo documentary, how about you tell me why you're here?" The intensity of his stare ruffled her stomach.

Macy swallowed and lifted her chin. "In that case, if you must know. I want an acting career. A real one, where I make a living. I have enough acting experience. I believe I have something to offer." Her words came out more defiant than she'd intended, but there it was... her God's honest truth.

Westwood raised his brows. "Now *that* I believe."

"Okay then. Thank you for the opportunity to audition." She punctuated it with a quick zip of her parka, grabbed her oversized purse, and headed for the door.

"Thanks for coming in," he said evenly with a quick nod.

Disappointment burned through Macy as she hurried down the carpeted hallway of the midtown Anchorage office building. She exited onto the sidewalk leading to the parking lot on Northern Lights Boulevard, where ten-degree air assaulted her senses—a reminder that January was ready to hand off its torch of subarctic chill to February. She stepped across the patchy ice to her car.

A nosy raven perched atop a light pole sent cheerful, musical clicks down to her as if to say, "Don't worry, honey, you've got this." He followed up with a gurgling croak.

Macy looked up warily. "Thanks, Mr. Nevermore. Please don't drop a gift on my windshield." Raven turds on a windshield at ten degrees had a way of hardening like petrified wood.

She berated herself for her botched audition. Though the Westwood guy had been terse, Macy knew better than to burn bridges. She'd wanted a role in this movie, ever since the announcement on local news. Film acting classes had filled her schedule outside of work, and she'd practiced reading lines with any warm body she could find. She'd even practiced lines while driving around town.

She figured it would have been easier to start her career in Alaska before pursuing opportunities in Los Angeles. Down there, she'd be another in a long line of aspiring actors, working odd jobs and waiting for a breakout role. In the meantime, she'd likely be waiting tables, cleaning toilets, or vacuuming heaven knows what from a porn actor's pool.

In Alaska, she could have distinguished herself. But her hopes went up in flames with her botched audition for Mr. Congeniality. Macy thought of Westwood's no-nonsense expression. She'd grown accustomed to working in a mostly male environment in her federal agency and was used to dealing with the occasional grumpy sunshine, but this guy didn't even give her a chance.

And there wasn't any hint of sunshine. Not even grumpy sunshine.

More like a cranky polar bear... with attitude.

*Everybody Loves Polar Bears*[2]

---

2. https://www.amazon.com/Everybody-Loves-Polar-Bears-Romantic-ebook/dp/
B0CQN356BC

# Polar Creek Christmas Recipes!

## Polar Creek Halibut Olympia

*Ingredients*

1 1/2 lbs. halibut fillet

1 sweet onion, sliced

1 tbsp. butter

1/2 cup mayonnaise

1/2 tbsp. Dijon mustard

1/2 cup plain Greek yogurt

1 tsp. dill weed

1/2 tsp. lemon juice

1/2 tsp. Worcestershire sauce

1/4 tsp. Tabasco (optional)

1 cup Panko bread crumbs

1/4 cup shaved or shredded parmesan cheese

1 tsp. chopped parsley

1/4 tsp. paprika

1/4 cup melted butter

*Directions:* Heat 1 tablespoon of butter in saucepan over medium heat. Add sliced onion until caramelized, about eight minutes. Mix mayonnaise, mustard, dill weed, sour cream, lemon juice, Worcestershire sauce, and Tabasco sauce. Set aside. Mix bread crumbs, parmesan cheese, parsley, paprika, and melted butter. Set aside. Arrange caramelized onion at bottom of casserole or baking dish. Layer halibut fillets on top of onions. Next, layer with mayonnaise mix. Top with bread-crumb mix. Bake at 350 degrees for ten to twelve minutes or until meat is flaky.

L oLo's Alaskan Salmon Dip
*Ingredients*

2 Alaskan sockeye salmon fillets, OR 1 six-ounce can of sockeye or pink salmon

1 tub of Smoked Salmon Philadelphia Cream Cheese

½ cup plain Greek yogurt (I use *Fage* nonfat)

½ fresh lime, squeezed

Himalayan sea salt or other salt to taste

1 tsp. capers in the jar and fresh parsley (optional)

*Directions:* If you use fresh or frozen salmon, bake it first. Be sure frozen fillets are thawed. Place in baking dish, skin side down, cover, and bake 20-25 minutes at 350 degrees. OR you can use canned salmon, as long as it's Alaska wild salmon and not that mushy Atlantic stuff. If using canned be sure to drain it or dip will be too runny. Cool baked salmon and chop into small pieces. I break it up with my fingers. Soften the salmon flavored cream cheese and add to a mixing bowl. Add the yogurt and mix well until creamy. Add salmon, lime juice, and capers and mix together. Add salt sparingly to taste. Put mixture into a serving dish and top with chopped parsley. Sometimes I lightly sprinkle paprika to give it a festive look. Chill and serve with chips or crackers.

## Praise For the Novels of LoLo Paige

"The strong women and smoking hot men who fight wildland fire, written by a lady who knows from personal experience. The books in this series are fiery page-turning reads."

*—Kat Martin, New York Times bestselling author*

"This series is cinematically plotted in spectacular, dangerous settings with a smoldering passion where fire isn't the only heat!" *—Cherry Adair, New York Times bestselling author*

"*Alaska Spark* is a feel-good love story, adventurous setting, and invigorating action combine to create a fresh romance novel that features a strong-willed yet troubled heroine, who the reader can't help but root for." *—Publishers Weekly Booklife Prize*

"*Alaska Inferno's* many storylines create a maelstrom of excitement. The poems bookending the narrative show its literary foundation. With a hopeful and happy conclusion, Paige successfully crafts a romance replete with adventure, whodunit intrigue, and art to suit many tastes. Paige's *Alaska Spark* was a 2021 Eric Hoffer Book Awards as an ebook fiction honorable mention."

*—U.S. Review of Books*

**The Blazing Hearts Wildfire Series**

Want more romantic reads? Here's what's heating up with my wildland firefighters! If you like romantic suspense, check out these books. Each novel is a standalone and doesn't have to be read in order.

*Alaska Spark*
*Alaska Inferno*
*Alaska Blaze*
*Alaska Firestorm*
*Alaska Flame*

Ignite your senses with the fearless women on the Aurora Fire Crew, who battle raging infernos in Alaska's untamed wilderness. This heart-pounding suspense series weaves passion, danger, and redemption as these extraordinary wildland firefighters confront personal demons as they fight wildfires. As these brave women work alongside equally courageous men—from daring smokejumpers to seasoned incident commanders—our heroines navigate a world where flames and desires burn equally fierce. Dive into these standalone books brimming with suspense, scorching romance, and the raw beauty of the Land of the Midnight Sun.

Workplace romances
Alpha male protectors,
Strong female firefighters
Friends to lovers & enemies to lovers,
Friendship alliances
First responders in small towns
Romantic suspense in Alaska's spectacular settings
Sabotage and danger with life-or-death stakes

Download *Alaska Dawn*, the FREE prequel to *Alaska Spark* by joining my VIP Readers List at *LoLoPaige.com*[1]

---

1. *https://www.lolopaige.com/*

# About the Author

LoLo Paige is an award-winning author in both romantic comedy and romantic suspense. Her action-adventure, romantic suspense books about wildland firefighting have topped the Amazon Bestseller Lists in the U.S., Canada, and Australia. The Blazing Hearts Wildfire series books have received several indie awards for best romance. Publishers Weekly has featured her books, and as a former wildland firefighter, LoLo's true story about escaping a runaway wildfire in Alaska's dangerous Interior won a 2016 Alaska Press Club award.

Want to connect and learn more about my books? Follow me on Amazon, Instagram, and Bluesky!

Did you love *Flights, Fights, & Christmas Lights*? Then you should read *Everybody Loves Polar Bears*[1] by LoLo Paige!

[2]

In the frosty mayhem of the Alaskan film set for Everybody Loves Polar Bears, accident-prone Macy Applegate catapults herself into a hilarious array of mishaps better suited for a blooper reel. As Macy dreams of stardom, she reluctantly works with Nick Westwood, the grumpiest and most arrogant assistant director this side of the Arctic Circle—a man who irritates her more than a stuck zipper in a sub-zero wind chill.

Beneath Nick's stoic exterior lies a mysterious secret, and the only thing more challenging than Alaska's winter is these

---

1. https://books2read.com/u/4jEZKY

2. https://books2read.com/u/4jEZKY

two trying to get along for longer than a commercial break. Macy is a walking disaster in matters of the heart, and Nick is fed up with shallow relationships. But fate has a penchant for mischief when Nick transforms from Macy's nemesis to her off-screen hero, chipping away at the permafrost around her heart. Should she give this guy a chance or continue wishing on the magical aurora borealis for perfect love?

In this hilarious romantic comedy, where polar bears play supporting roles and love takes center stage, Macy and Nick navigate a situation as unpredictable as Macy's on-set blunders. If you swooned through The Proposal and chuckled at The Hating Game...and if you have a soft spot for polar bears...get ready for laughter in this heartwarming tale of unexpected love.

Read more at https://www.lolopaige.com.